It was all n  **d frightening.**

Maybe what those ~~~~ eyes were doing to her heart rate was the most frightening of all.

"Stop worrying," Nick said, obviously sensing her anxiety.

Cara swallowed, realizing that he knew exactly what she'd been thinking. She wasn't normally that transparent. Not with men. Of course, he wasn't exactly the kind of man she was used to dealing with, either.

"Then...what are you talking about?"

That's it. Pretend you don't know. Ask to be embarrassed. Make a bigger fool of yourself than you already have.

"I'm not going to try to make love to you."

For some stupid reason she couldn't leave it alone. She couldn't just nod and walk across the room and crawl into her own bed like the chastened child she felt right now.

"I never thought you were."

Dear Harlequin Intrigue Reader,

To mark a month of fall festivals, screeching goblins and hot apple cider, Harlequin Intrigue has a provocative October lineup guaranteed to spice things up!

Debra Webb launches her brand-new spin-off series, COLBY AGENCY: INTERNAL AFFAIRS, with *Situation: Out of Control.* This first installment sets the stage for the most crucial mission of all…smoking out a mole in their midst. The adrenaline keeps flowing in *Rules of Engagement* by acclaimed author Gayle Wilson, who continues her PHOENIX BROTHERHOOD series with a gripping murder mystery that hurls an unlikely couple into a vortex of danger.

Also this month, a strictly business arrangement turns into a lethal attraction, in *Cowboy Accomplice* by B.J. Daniels—book #2 in her Western series, McCALLS' MONTANA. And just in time for Halloween, October's haunting ECLIPSE selection, *The Legacy of Croft Castle* by Jean Barrett, promises to put you in that spooky frame of mind.

There are more thrills to come when Kara Lennox unveils the next story in her CODE OF THE COBRA series, with *Bounty Hunter Redemption,* which pits an alpha male lawman against a sexy parole officer when mayhem strikes. And, finally this month, watch for the action-packed political thriller *Shadow Soldier* by talented newcomer Dana Marton. This debut book spotlights an antiterrorist operative who embarks on a high-stakes mission to dismantle a diabolical ticking time bomb.

Enjoy!

Denise O'Sullivan
Senior Editor
Harlequin Intrigue

RULES OF ENGAGEMENT

GAYLE WILSON

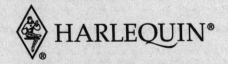

HARLEQUIN®

TORONTO • NEW YORK • LONDON
AMSTERDAM • PARIS • SYDNEY • HAMBURG
STOCKHOLM • ATHENS • TOKYO • MILAN • MADRID
PRAGUE • WARSAW • BUDAPEST • AUCKLAND

ISBN 0-373-22802-3

RULES OF ENGAGEMENT

ABOUT THE AUTHOR

Five-time RITA® Award finalist and RITA® Award winner Gayle Wilson has written over thirty novels and three novellas for Harlequin/Silhouette. She has received more than forty awards and nominations for her work.

Gayle still lives in Alabama, where she was born, with her husband of thirty-four years. She loves to hear from readers. Write to her at P.O. Box 3277, Hueytown, AL 35023. Visit Gayle online at www.booksbygaylewilson.com.

Books by Gayle Wilson

*Home to Texas
†Men of Mystery
††More Men of Mystery
**Phoenix Brotherhood

FOR YOUR EYES ONLY

CIA AGENT PROFILE

Name: Nick Morelli

Date of birth: October 31, 1967

Assigned Team: External Security

Special Skills: Trained in counterterrorism; airborne qualified; desert, mountain and jungle survival training; fluent in Russian; hand-to-hand combat expert; expert marksman.

Agent Evaluation: Although this ex-ranger is clearly a loner by inclination, he has proven on numerous occasions to be an invaluable asset to the external security team. His courage and intelligence continue to place him in the top echelon of operatives.

Status: Identity Erased

Current Address: The Phoenix Brotherhood

FOR YOUR EYES ONLY

CAST OF CHARACTERS

Nick Morelli—The lone wolf Phoenix operative becomes involved in an investigation that is very personal. Did his estranged father really commit suicide or did something—and someone—from his past finally catch up to him?

Cara Simonson—Cara has accepted her father's death as a terrible accident—until Nick Morelli shows up at his wake, asking questions for which she has no answers. Cara recognizes that the dark and dangerous Phoenix agent is outside the bounds of her experience, but she can't resist the man—or the mission he's on.

Griff Cabot—Any time one of his agents is in trouble, Griff and all the resources of the Phoenix are always available. This time, however, Cabot learns almost too late that the hunter has now become the hunted.

Miriam Simonson—Cara's mother would give anything to know that her husband hadn't been driven to start drinking again, but does she have any useful knowledge of events that took place more than thirty-five years ago and thousands of miles away?

Duncan McGregor—Was McGregor another innocent victim or the ghost from the past who is haunting their lives?

Richard Ainsworth—The FBI's assistant executive director claims that the special agent who contacted Nick's father left no record of the contact and had no reason to be interested in Vincent Morelli.

Jack Davis—Does Davis hold the key to the mystery? If so, can Nick and Cara reach him before he becomes the next victim?

Colonel Ron Kittering—What happened in a Vietnamese jungle more than thirty-five years ago is a secret too many people now know. Is Kittering one of them?

To the officers and the men
of the 174th Assault Helicopter Unit,
who served both honorably and with great valor.

And to my own hero, Shark 9.

Prologue

"It's personal business," Nick Morelli said.

The man seated on the other side of Griff Cabot's mahogany desk seemed uneasy, like a coiled steel spring ready to explode. Maybe that was because Nick had so rarely been in his office, Griff realized with a sense of surprise. In all the years they'd worked together, he couldn't remember Nick coming here other than to receive an assignment or for an after-mission debriefing.

One of the original members of the External Security Team, Nick Morelli had always been a loner. He still was, Cabot acknowledged, studying the rugged face of the man he'd known for almost a decade.

Nick had become an Army Ranger straight out of high school, working his way up through the ranks. Based on his record and his intellect, he'd been tapped for Army Intelligence and eventually recruited by the CIA. He had also been one of the first operatives Griff had chosen when he had formed his elite covert operations team more than ten years ago.

Despite their long association, Cabot realized that he knew virtually nothing about Nick's personal life.

He didn't think he'd ever heard him mention family or even where he was from. Morelli was very much a closed book. And obviously that was the way he wanted it.

His black hair was still militarily short, although it was now touched lightly with gray at the temples. The gaze from the dark brown eyes was exactly as it had always been—level and unflinching. Despite the fact that he must be in his midthirties, Nick appeared to be in good enough physical condition that Cabot wouldn't have bet against him being able to pass the same rigorous physical the Rangers had required when he'd enlisted at eighteen.

"How much time will you need?"

"A week at the outside," Nick said. "All the loose ends on the Palmer case have been tied up, or I wouldn't ask."

Whatever this request for personal leave was about, Griff probably would never have heard about it if Nick hadn't been without an assignment right now. Cabot realized that in itself was unusual. Nick Morelli was always the first to volunteer. Even in the days of the External Security Team he had been, no matter the extent of danger the mission had involved.

"When's the last time you took leave, Nick?"

The brown eyes remained locked on his face, the thinned lips unmoving.

"I can look it up," Cabot said after the silence stretched uncomfortably.

"After Basra."

Basra, an EST mission to rescue one of their own, had occurred…more than seven years ago, Griff realized, quickly doing the math. And the time off Nick had taken after it had been for medical reasons.

"Then I think you're due for some downtime. Why don't you take a couple of weeks?"

"This won't take me that long."

Nick was normally reticent, but there was something about the tone of that clipped pronouncement that troubled Griff. He had been reading men for a long time, even ones like this—tough and brave and very private, especially when it came to anything that involved their emotions. In spite of Nick's attempt to downplay his request for time off, there was something in his eyes that made Griff guess that whatever was going on with one of his best operatives was, indeed, deeply emotional.

"Let me know if there's anything the Phoenix can do to help," Griff offered.

The resulting lift at one corner of Nick's lips was as close to a smile as Cabot could remember seeing on his face. He hid it as he got to his feet, his posture as ramrod straight as if he were still in the army. Griff found himself waiting for the requisite salute.

"Just don't replace me while I'm gone," Nick said instead.

Griff's answering smile was far more open. "Is that why you've never taken time off, Nick? Because you were afraid I'd replace you?"

"I never took leave because there's never been anything I'd rather be doing than what I've done for you."

"And now there is?"

The silence after his question again lasted several seconds. "Believe me, Griff," Nick said with a conviction so heartfelt it left no room for doubt, "I'd rather be doing almost *anything* other than this."

Without any further explanation of that cryptic statement, Nick turned and walked across the room to the office door. His hand had already closed around the knob when Griff's question stopped him.

"Are you sure there's nothing I can do to help?"

Cabot had almost let it go, but again there was something about Nick's tone that bothered him. He knew his operative wouldn't appreciate his concern, but that was truly what had prompted the question.

Nick turned, those dark eyes holding on Griff's face a moment before he said, "If you have a special relationship with any of the saints, you could say a prayer for an old soldier who needs one."

The request was so out of character that it rendered Griff speechless for the few vital seconds it took for Nick to open the door and disappear through it.

...you could say a prayer for an old soldier who needs one.

Nick? Although he had been a soldier, the "old" part didn't seem to apply. If the phrase had been a reference to someone else, however, Griff didn't have a clue as to whom.

Long after that brief meeting had ended, the words would come back to haunt the founder of the Phoenix, echoing in his head with a troubling despair. As a result, on more than one occasion during the remainder of the afternoon, Cabot invoked a power far higher than he possessed, asking Him to watch over Nick Morelli.

Chapter One

Littleford, Mississippi

Nick Morelli opened the door with the key his father's lawyer had given him. He stood in the entryway a moment, letting the memories wash over him in an unforgiving wave of regret.

It must have been at least three years since he'd been here, yet it seemed that nothing in the small house had changed. The ceiling fan was on, its low creak the only sound in the late afternoon stillness. Sunlight slanted into the front room, highlighting dust motes that floated upward in the draft from the slow-moving blades.

Nick took a breath and stepped inside, closing the door behind him. He didn't want to be here. Certainly not less than two hours after his father's funeral. But he had told himself that the quicker he sorted through the things in this house, the quicker he'd be able to get back to work. And that was something he very much wanted.

He walked over to his father's battered recliner, aligned directly in front of the TV screen. Nick put his hand on the headrest, the slow movement of his fingers over its cracked vinyl almost a caress. He swallowed the same ache of emotion he had fought during the graveside service, forcing his stinging eyes to survey his surroundings. Trying to decide on the best place to start.

Maybe with the items that cluttered the small table to the left of the chair. In easy reach for anyone sitting there were the TV remote and a half-empty cup of coffee, stone-cold, of course, after four days. A folded section of newspaper had been propped against the mug. The rest of it was scattered on the floor.

A ballpoint pen lay on top of a stack of opened mail, the envelopes raggedly ripped across one end. There were also several loose sheets of paper, torn from a nearby pad. Each held a line or two of writing or a numbered list in his father's bold, easily recognizable block printing.

Everything in the house would have to be gone through. Bills paid. Utilities cut off. Correspondents notified. And the hardest of all, some final disposition of his father's belongings arranged.

Nick could have paid someone to do those things—something he could well afford—but on some level he knew that *he* needed to do them. An act of penance, maybe. For not coming back often enough. For the quality of their relationship. Most of all for having had no idea his father was going to take his service revolver, put it into his mouth, and pull the trigger.

He blocked the image, infinitely grateful the suicide hadn't taken place inside this house, but in the small toolshed out back. If it had been here, that would have made the task he'd set for himself far harder than it already was. And God knew it was going to be difficult enough.

No reason not to start here, he decided, looking

down on the pile on the cluttered table. He couldn't
bring himself to sit down in the recliner, so he gathered up the mail and pieces of paper and carried them
over to the breakfast bar, which served as a divider between the den and the tiny kitchen. He pulled out one
of the stools and laid the stack on the counter.

As he did, he noticed that the light on the answering machine, which sat at one end of the counter, was
blinking. Its small, almost baleful red eye winked off
and on, nagging him, now that he'd noticed it, like a
toothache.

He sat down on the stool and reluctantly reached
over to punch the play button. According to the tape,
there were four new messages. As he listened to the
first, an advertisement for a local aluminum siding in-
staller, he picked up the top envelope in the stack and
slid its contents out through the torn end.

Last month's electric bill, for a grand total of $87.54.
He set the notice and its return envelope off to the side.
He had already picked up the next bill when the first
words of the second message caused his hands to hesi-
tate.

"Don Crawford, Sergeant Morelli. I wanted to con-
firm that, as per our conversation on Monday, I'll be
in Littleford tomorrow. I'll see you at five. Please
bring whatever documentation you have." According
to the date at the end of the message, it had been left
the day after his father's death.

Sergeant Morelli? His dad hadn't been Sergeant
Morelli in more than twenty years.

Nick laid down the envelope and pressed the
rewind button. The old-fashioned tape whirled back
through the two messages he had already heard. When
it clicked off, he pushed Play, listening to them again.

The second one made no more sense this time than it had before. The only thing that was clear was that his father had made an appointment to meet someone two days after his suicide. An appointment he apparently hadn't bothered to call and cancel before he blew his brains out.

Macabre. Almost laughable. Except none of this had been remotely amusing. Not the call he'd received about his father or having to ask Griff for time off or the hurried flight to Mississippi. Certainly not identifying the body at the morgue and making arrangements for his dad's burial.

Nick was no stranger to death. Not in any of its guises. He had lost friends both in the military and on Cabot's External Security Team. Some of those men had been closer than brothers.

The losses were to be expected, given that the covert missions they had handled were always dangerous. They all knew and accepted the risks. His father's death, however...

Again Nick imposed the rigid self-control that had gotten him through the ceremony. This was almost finished. All he had to do was to take care of his father's personal business and then get on the next plane back to Washington.

In the meantime, he should probably try to get in touch with Don Crawford. At least let him know why his dad hadn't shown up for that meeting.

There hadn't been a phone number on the message tape, but there might be one in the stuff he'd picked up off the table. He began to sort through it, laying the envelopes that obviously contained bills on top of the payment stack he'd begun without bothering to look at their contents.

He paused in his methodical sorting only when he came to an envelope that had nothing written on the front and no stamp. When he turned it over, he discovered that it hadn't been sealed.

He tilted the contents toward the open flap and a dozen or so snapshots slid onto his palm. The top one was of his dad. A much younger version. And in uniform.

Still holding the envelope, Nick began to go through the pictures, looking at each and then slipping it to the back of the stack. It became clear by the third or fourth photograph that these had all been taken in Vietnam.

Most were posed shots—young, crew-cut soldiers in their late teens or early twenties, smiling into the camera. There were a few older men, probably officers, although the prints were small enough that it was impossible to distinguish insignia.

And almost equally impossible to distinguish faces, he realized. Without differences in hairstyles or clothing, the smiling features seemed to blend together.

Nick compared a couple of pictures, holding them side by side to try to figure out if they contained any of the same people. Other than his father and a heavyset, dark-haired kid, the GIs were practically indistinguishable.

He couldn't imagine why his dad had had these beside his chair. His father never talked about 'Nam. He wasn't one of those who went to reunions or told war stories. It was as if that year of his life had never existed.

Now, in the days before his suicide, he had arranged a meeting with someone who called him Sergeant Morelli and had these photographs beside his chair.

Maybe he had pulled them out to show the Crawford guy.

Giving up on the mystery, at least temporarily, Nick laid the snapshots and their envelope down on the counter. Then he picked up the untidy stack of pages that had been torn from the notepad. He glanced at each, discarding them as if he were dealing cards.

One was obviously a grocery list. Another some kind of "to-do" reminders, which included the notation "Pick up laundry on Monday."

Monday. Two days after his father's suicide. The same day he was supposed to meet Crawford. It seemed obvious that when his father had complied this reminder list and made that appointment, he hadn't been planning on taking his own life.

Somewhere inside Nick's gut a niggling sense that there was something wrong with that scenario had begun to grow. He ignored it, resolutely returning to the papers from the notepad.

The third sheet contained a list of names. It started with "Me" and then listed five other people, first names or what appeared to be nicknames only. Nick didn't recognize any of them.

On a hunch, he thumbed back through the photographs. None of them matched the list. There were no groups of six. And in none of the pictures was his father at the left, which would seem to be indicated by the order of the listing he'd made. The obvious conclusion was that the names on that sheet weren't intended to identify people in one of the pictures.

Then what the hell were they?

And who the hell was Don Crawford? The need to get in touch with him, if only to inform him of why his father didn't keep the appointment they'd made, brought Nick's attention back to the few remaining sheets.

A couple had words jotted on them that he couldn't make heads or tails of. On the last was the notation "The Cypresses" and under that was what looked like a phone number.

The Cypresses was a well-known restaurant in a larger town about fifty miles down the interstate. Its reputation was such that people from Littleford frequently drove down for dinner. His father, however, had never cared that much about good food, certainly not enough to make a hundred-mile round-trip to get it.

The significant part, as far as Nick was concerned, was the unfamiliar phone number. The state had recently been divided into a couple of newly created area codes. It was possible, he supposed, that the number might be that of the restaurant.

Maybe his dad had called for reservations. Maybe he was going to stand Don Crawford to a good meal, as out of character as that would be. The image of Vincent Morelli assuming the role of some bon vivant host provoked a small, almost twisted smile on the lips of his son.

There was only one way to find out, Nick decided, reaching for the receiver. The number he dialed rang three times before the call was answered. The speaker immediately identified the number he'd reached, which wasn't, as it turned out, The Cypresses restaurant.

"Federal Bureau of Investigation. May I help you?"

A half dozen scenarios ran through Nick's mind. None of them adequately explained why his father would have the FBI's number written on a sheet of paper beside his chair. None other than the obvious one, which was that he had called them.

On a hunch, Nick said, "I'm trying to get in touch with Don Crawford."

There was a fraction of a second's hesitation before the female voice on the other end responded. "Is this about an ongoing investigation?"

Was it? Again, operating totally in the dark, Nick went with his gut.

"Yes, it is. Is he available?"

"Hold on, please, while I connect you with the special agent who is now handling Agent Crawford's cases."

After perhaps thirty seconds a masculine voice answered. "Special Agent Bennett. I understand that you're calling about a case that Special Agent Crawford was handling?"

"Actually, I was just trying to touch base with Don. We went to school together, but we'd lost touch. I thought maybe I could reach him through the Bureau, which was where he was the last time we talked. Has he left?"

Nothing like making it up as you go along, Nick thought. He figured that Agent Bennett might give more information in response to a personal inquiry than to someone connected with an investigation.

"I'm sorry to have to be the bearer of bad news, but I guess I'm not surprised you haven't heard. Don passed away a couple of days ago."

"Passed away?"

The shock in Nick's voice wasn't feigned. A couple of days ago meant that Special Agent Crawford had died on the same day he'd arranged to meet with Nick's father. And only two days after his dad's suicide. That niggling uneasiness in the pit of his stomach had grown into full-throttle alarm.

"Massive coronary. Shocked the hell out of everyone here, I can tell you."

"Coronary. My God," Nick said, remembering his story about their having gone to school together. "He was my age."

"Forty-one. Unbelievable. Looked to be in as good a shape as anyone here. I guess you never can tell."

"Isn't that the truth?"

"If you'd like to leave your name and number," Bennett offered, "I'll pass the message on to Janelle. I can't give you her number because of regulations. Hope you understand."

"Of course. Actually, I'm only in town tonight on my way out of the country. I'd hoped to catch up with Don and take him to dinner. Talk about old times. I can't believe I won't ever be able to do that again. It's gonna take me a while to adjust to that."

"I know how you feel. Let me know if you want to get in touch with the family. What did you say your name was again?"

Apparently Bennett was getting his professional equilibrium back. Although he had given Nick no information that wouldn't be a matter of public record, he also hadn't properly verified the individual to whom he was giving it.

"Robert Jones," Nick said without hesitation. Every school on the planet had a Bob Jones enrolled.

"And you say you went to college with Don?"

"High school," he said, making it more difficult for Bennett if he decided to check. "A very *long* time ago. Look, despite the nature of the news, I really appreciate you sharing it with me. I'm gonna go out and lift a few in memory of Don. He was a good man. Thanks."

"And your number—"

Nick pushed the button on the receiver, breaking the connection. Of course, if the guy wanted, he could probably track down the number from which the call was made, but the phone was in his father's name.

Which was apparently already in an FBI file somewhere. In a file belonging to an agent who was also dead.

Nick had been in the intelligence business too long not to be bothered by that kind of coincidence. Maybe he just didn't want to accept his father's suicide, but something about this whole setup was beginning to smell.

His eyes fell back to the envelope containing the Vietnam-era photos. He dumped them out on the breakfast counter, his fingers separating them. Too many things didn't add up, especially his father's newly awakened interest in his days in Vietnam and his return to being Sergeant Morelli.

Nick slid the list of names over beside the snapshots. Me, Hiram, Scottie, John, Buddy, The Shark.

He still had contacts within the Department of the Army. Some very good friends still worked in intel, including the man who'd recruited him. Maybe it was time to call in a few favors.

Chapter Two

All funerals, of necessity, have certain elements in common. Nick was finding this one, however, to be far too close for comfort to the last he'd attended.

He forced his gaze away from the tight blue triangle of the folded flag to focus on the woman to whom it was being presented. Softened by age and marked now by grief, her features still managed to convey an unyielding strength of character.

Good bones, his mother would have said.

Those were reflected in the face of her daughter, as well. Striking rather than beautiful, Cara Simonson was one of those women who would always turn heads.

Dressed in a simple navy sheath, she had secured her sun-streaked blond hair into a low chignon on the back of her neck. The severity of the style emphasized that same classic bone structure, which lay under pale, flawless skin.

Like her mother's, her face gave evidence of the strain the last few days had been. The blue eyes were circled by smudges of exhaustion.

Nick felt a surge of empathy for the women. He understood all too well the emotional toll this was taking on them. His own loss was still an open wound, especially given what he'd discovered about his father's death. Attending another military funeral had not been a remedy for that pain.

In the midst of that now-familiar reverie, he became aware suddenly that the service had ended. The mourners at the edge of the crowd had already begun to drift away, walking in groups of two or three across the carefully manicured lawn to their waiting cars. Those who had stood nearest the family were offering final condolences, most addressed to the younger of the Simonson women.

Nick's eyes again considered her face, looking for something of the man they had buried today. Whatever Cara Simonson had inherited from her father, it wasn't revealed in those nearly patrician features.

I hope to hell that what you got instead was his courage, he thought. *I've got a feeling that before this is over you're going to need it.*

NO ONE QUESTIONED his right to be at the Simonson home. No more than they had questioned his right to attend the funeral. A couple who had been leaving the two-story colonial as he came up the walk had nodded at him as if they thought they knew him.

None of them did. The closest he'd ever been to West Virginia was flying over it on his way in and out of Washington. And his only connection to this family was the man they had just left behind at the cemetery.

The crowd inside had begun to thin by the time Nick walked through the front door. His timing was perfect for what he intended. Enough people were left that he should be able to blend in without calling attention to himself, yet there were so few that he could wait them out if he had to.

All he needed was five minutes alone with Cara Simonson. His impressions at the cemetery had cemented his choice, especially given her unique qualifications for the job ahead. If they hadn't, he wasn't sure what he would have done next.

"A real tragedy."

Nick turned his head, realizing the man at his elbow had directed the comment to him.

"Prime of life," the guy added when he saw he had Nick's attention.

"Yeah. A shame," Nick responded, pointedly returning his attention to the rest of the crowd.

As he did, he caught sight of Cara. She was on the other side of the dining room, her back to him, deep in conversation with an elderly couple. The white-haired man was holding her hand, occasionally patting the top of it, while his wife leaned forward earnestly, talking nonstop.

Nick was willing to bet that under normal circumstances Cara would have welcomed a rescue. In this case, however, there was no doubt that whatever those two were saying was going to be more palatable than what he had come to tell her.

"They say he'd been drinking again." Despite Nick's attempt to signal an end to the conversation, the man beside him seemed determined to share his insight on what had happened to Hiram Simonson. "Must have made it hard on Miriam after all these years. Once a drunk, always a drunk, I guess."

"So they say," Nick said.

That was information he hadn't gleaned from the

description of the accident in the local papers. He filed it away for future reference because the group he'd been watching showed signs of breaking up. Cara Simonson's hand had been released, and the older woman was putting hers in the crook of her companion's arm.

"Excuse me," Nick said to his informant. "Need to pay my respects."

The gaze of the man beside him followed his. "Easy on the eyes, isn't she?"

Despite the fact that Nick had thought essentially the same thing during the funeral, there was something about the remark that seemed inappropriate. Choosing to ignore it, he nodded a curt dismissal before he moved forward. The older couple passed him, making their way toward the front door.

"Ms. Simonson?"

She turned in response to her name. It was obvious from her eyes that she was trying to place him.

"Thank you for coming," she said, giving up and holding out her hand.

"Did you know your father had started drinking again?"

Her eyes widened. The involuntary reaction was followed by a slow flush of color, which seeped under the translucence of her skin, staining her neck before moving into her cheeks.

"Who the hell *are* you?" she demanded, all pretense at politeness gone.

"I'm Vince Morelli's son."

She waited, but deliberately he said nothing else. "Is that supposed to mean something to me?"

"I think it would have meant something to your father."

Her lips were still slightly parted from the shock of the question he'd asked. After a few seconds, she closed them, pressing them together so tightly that they whitened. When she spoke again, her voice was very soft.

"In case you haven't noticed, Mr. Morelli, my father's dead."

She started to walk past him, but he took her arm, turning her to draw her toward the French doors that led out onto a small sunroom. He managed two or three steps before she stopped, resisting his attempt to urge her forward.

"What do you think you're doing?"

Her voice was pitched low enough not to attract the attention of the others in the room. He had been counting on her unwillingness to make a scene, as well as on the element of surprise, to get her alone. She had recovered more quickly than he'd anticipated.

"I'm trying to give you some information about your father's death. Something I doubt you'll want broadcast to the people in there."

His fingers were still wrapped around her upper arm. Hers had begun to pull at them. With those words, they stopped.

Her eyes came up, searching his face. Nick waited, almost watching the thoughts move behind those dark blue irises.

After a few seconds she let her hand fall, no longer prying at his fingers. As soon as she began to move toward the glassed-in porch, he freed her arm and followed.

When he reached the doorway, he glanced over his shoulder. There were only a few people in the front rooms now, and none of them seemed to be paying the slightest attention to the two of them. As he entered the sunroom, Cara Simonson turned, her face reflecting the same anger he had heard in her voice.

"What's this all about?"

He had mentally rehearsed on the plane how to begin. When it came down to it, however, Nick did what he always did. He went with his gut. He wasn't good at doctoring things up. He had always shot straight from the hip. Something he'd learned from his dad, he realized with a stab of remorse.

"Your father's death wasn't an accident."

Whatever Cara Simonson had been expecting him to say, clearly it wasn't that. Her lips parted again, as if she were about to respond. After a moment she closed them, her gaze lifting to focus somewhere over his shoulder.

She was looking into the other room, he realized. Trying to judge if there was anyone else within hearing distance? Or only if her mother might be?

When her eyes came back to his, they were narrowed. "If you're from the insurance company—"

"I'm not. And I'm not from the police. I'm…an interested bystander."

A hell of a word choice, he acknowledged. Where her father was concerned, however, it was true. Rightly or wrongly, Nick wasn't here because of Hiram Simonson's death. It was too late to do anything about that.

"I don't know what you're after—"

"Your help," he interrupted. "I don't want anything else from you, I promise."

Her lips closed as she considered his face. Evaluating.

"What kind of help?"

The tone was grudging. As wary as her eyes.

He couldn't blame her. And what he was about to tell her wouldn't be easy to swallow. Not for anyone.

It would have been better if he could have waited a few days. Given her some time and distance. But if he was right about what was going on, waiting was a luxury he couldn't afford.

"I think your father was murdered."

The silence this time lasted through several heart-beats. From the front of the house came the sound of laughter. It seemed as incongruous in this setting as the words he'd just uttered.

"My father got drunk and drove his car off an embankment and into a tree," she said, her voice flat. "Whatever scam you're trying to pull isn't going to work. It was what they call an open-and-shut case."

He could read in her eyes the emotional exhaustion he'd glimpsed at the funeral. It was tinged now with disappointment, or maybe cynicism that someone would come to her dead father's home and try to con her.

"Did you have any indication before the accident that your father was drinking again?"

It was the same question he had posed when he'd approached her a few minutes ago. This time she thought about it. For all of ten seconds.

"My father was an alcoholic. Even when he *wasn't* drinking, he was one drink away from being drunk."

"So what made him take a drink that night?"

Another beat of silence.

"Who can know what makes an alcoholic take another drink? I can't remember any earth-shattering event that precipitated his previous falls off the wagon," she said bitterly.

"What I'm saying is maybe he *didn't* take this one. Not voluntarily."

Again her eyes examined his, almost as if she wanted to believe him. It was obvious by what she said next that logic had won out over that desire.

"We don't need this now. Whatever you're selling, we aren't buying. It doesn't matter what my father did or why he did it. He's dead. It's over. My mother and I just want to be left alone."

Nick wasn't far enough away from that exact feeling not to experience a rush of guilt for putting her through this. After all, *he* hadn't become convinced right away. Not until he had started trying to put things together and found that they didn't add up.

It wasn't fair to expect her to buy in just because he was so sure. The problem was he really *needed* her to buy into what he thought was going on. And to do it soon.

"If you'll let me show you what I've found—"

"Get out," she said. "Do it now before I get someone to throw you out."

Nick had the distinct impression that the need to get rid of him was about to outweigh the desire not to cause a scene.

"I'll be in town a couple of days," he said, keeping his voice controlled and his message rational. "All I'm asking is that you think about it. Think about everything. What happened that night. Your father's state of mind. Ask your mother why *she* thinks he took that drink. Whether he had any reason to. Then take a look at the police report. If you see anything that doesn't add up, anything that makes you think your dad might *not* have voluntarily driven his car into that tree, give me a call."

He reached into the breast pocket of his blazer and drew out his card, the one with the discreet graphic of the phoenix rising from flames. He held it out to her, but she made no move to take it.

"Think about it," he said again. "That's all I'm asking."

"Don't ever come here again," she said. "If you do, I'll call the police."

"Ask for the cop who did the on-site investigation of your father's accident," he advised. "Ask him if he noticed anything strange that night. After you've done that, you might want to look into what happened to Special Agent Don Crawford of the FBI."

He waited for her to walk away. That's all she had to do to put an end to this. Step past him and return to the front rooms where there were still a few visitors. And an escape from what he was asking of her.

She didn't move. Her eyes held his a long time. Then, when he'd almost given up hope, she reached out and took the card.

As she did, her fingers brushed his, sending an unexpected frisson of reaction through his body. She stepped past him, being careful not to touch him again.

Maybe that was just wishful thinking on his part, he admitted. Believing that she had been as conscious of that jolt of sensation as he'd been.

Wishful thinking. Just like believing she was ever going to dial the number on the card he'd just handed her.

Chapter Three

"Who was he?"

Cara looked up from the ham sandwich she had been toying with and into her mother's face. She appeared as exhausted as Cara felt.

"Who was who?"

She lifted one neatly cut quarter piece of sandwich and took a bite. She made herself chew and then swallow. It tasted like cardboard. Just as everything else she'd eaten during the last three days had.

"The man you were talking to out on the sunporch," her mother said patiently. "Navy blazer. Dark hair."

Tall, dark and dangerous. If ever that hackneyed phrase were appropriate...

"Oh, him," Cara said, maintaining the pretense that she hadn't known all along who her mother meant. "His father was a friend of Dad's."

"Who?"

Her mother's sandwich was still untouched, although she, too, was holding a quarter in her hand. Cara knew she would eventually eat it. Her mom was a firm believer in "carrying on."

"I think he said Morelli."

"They must have been close."

"He and Dad?"

"For the son to come to the funeral. Don't you think? I could understand the father coming, but sending the son? Above and beyond."

"I guess."

"Did he say why his father couldn't come?"

"I don't think he did," Cara said.

She took another bite of her sandwich, trying to think of some way to shift the conversation into another direction.

"Didn't you ask him?"

Cara shook her head, chewing to avoid having to answer.

"Good-looking," her mother said.

"What?"

"I thought he was good-looking."

"I didn't notice."

"It wouldn't hurt you to notice."

Her mother's goal in life for the last few years had been to see Cara happily married and producing grandchildren. Although she always professed a great deal of satisfaction with her life and her career, Cara knew that her professional ambitions weren't the real reason she hadn't lived up to her mother's dreams.

Throughout high school and college, she had always fallen into the "brains rather than beauty" category. Her natural shyness hadn't helped, of course. And being confronted with someone like Nick Morelli, so outside her realm of experience, made her feel like the same awkward, bookish teen her classmates had always considered her to be.

"Please don't start," Cara said.

If her mother wanted to play matchmaker, it shouldn't be with someone who created such a strong sense of anxiety in her stomach. And that was not only, she admitted, because of what he had suggested.

Her mother laughed, putting the still untouched sandwich back down on her plate. She had picked it up and put it down half a dozen times without taking a bite.

"Don't worry. I'm too tired to nag. I swear I feel as if I've been beaten. My mother always said funerals are endurance contests. You have to make conversation with dozens of people who would rather be anywhere else than there."

"And so would you, of course," Cara said.

"At least it's over. No more sacrifices to convention. We can both have hysterics and collapse in good conscience."

A small silence fell, the relaxed, natural kind that occurs between people so closely attuned they have no need of words. Her mother lifted another section of sandwich off her plate and brought it toward her mouth.

"Did anything happen that day?"

Cara couldn't believe she had said those words. Suddenly they had just been there between them, interrupting the companionship.

Her mother looked up, eyes questioning. "*What* day?"

"The day Daddy died. What happened to make him start drinking again?"

There was a pause, long enough that Cara had plenty of time to regret beginning this.

"Nothing," her mother said, moving her head slowly from side to side. "Not one thing out of the ordinary happened that day. Believe me, I've racked my brain trying to figure out what went wrong. Trying to see what it was that could have set him off. I always come back to the same thing."

"And what is that?"

"Nothing. I can't think of one single thing that would make your father take a drink. Not after six years. Maybe if I could…"

"If you could?" Cara prodded when the sentence trailed.

"Then maybe I could make sense of it. Why he would do that after all that time."

"Would it help?"

Her mother looked up, eyes widened in surprise. "Of course it would help. Now, it's just…an emptiness. Maybe if I understood the reason, there wouldn't be one."

"Even if you found out something you didn't want to know?"

"About your father?" Miriam Simonson laughed, the sound soft, almost nostalgic. "There wasn't anything about your father I wouldn't want to know. Especially now."

"I mean something…" Cara hesitated, searching for a word that wasn't cruel.

"Unsavory?" her mother supplied with a smile.

"What if there was something like that?"

"There wasn't. I can promise you that. But, yes, I'd want to know. Even about that. Then at least I'd know it wasn't me. Us. I'd know he wasn't tired of what we had."

"Mom." The single syllable was a protest.

"That's what they were all thinking. Didn't you see it in their eyes?"

Cara hadn't, but then she wasn't the one who had been looking for it. Not the one dreading to find judgment in their expressions of sympathy.

"Of course not. And if you thought you did, it was your imagination."

"*You* didn't wonder?"

"About you and Dad? Never."

"Then why ask if anything happened?"

"Because *something* had to. *Something* had to have happened that day. Didn't it?"

"I guess so." Her mother picked up the piece of sandwich again, bringing it almost to her mouth before she added softly, her eyes welling with the tears she had managed to control until now, "And I'd give almost anything to know what it was."

"I DID WHAT YOU told me."

Although more than twenty-four hours had passed since he'd heard it, Nick had no trouble recognizing the voice on the phone. He shifted his cell to the other ear, sitting up on the side of the bed and reaching for the pad and pen the motel had thoughtfully provided on the bedside table.

"You found something." He was careful to keep the excitement out of his voice.

"I need to talk to you," Cara Simonson said. "Is there somewhere we could meet?"

"Where are you?"

"At my parents' house. My mother's house," she corrected. "But I don't want you to come here. I haven't told her what you said."

And she sure as hell wasn't going to agree to come to his room. She'd want somewhere public. Given the situation, he couldn't blame her.

"Is there a restaurant close to you? Something near the interstate?"

There was no hesitation in her reply, which made him believe she'd already thought out all of the arrangements.

"You remember the exit you took from the cemetery?"

"Yeah."

"There's a place called Carly's. On the right off the ramp."

"Half an hour?"

"I'll see you there."

As soon as she voiced her agreement, she broke the connection. No goodbye. No small talk.

Whatever Cara Simonson had discovered, it hadn't made her inclined to consider him her new best friend. Which was okay with Nick. It wasn't her friendship he needed.

As soon as Nick pulled off the access road, he spotted the silver Mercedes that had been parked in the Simonsons' driveway yesterday. It was glaringly out of place at the barbecue shack she'd directed him to. Chosen because she could be sure no one she knew would be dining here?

As Nick turned into the parking lot, he realized Cara was still sitting in the driver's seat of the car. Judging by the restaurant's clientele, gathered on benches at the front to wait for tables, he couldn't blame her for being reluctant to venture in on her own.

Through the windshield of the Mercedes, her eyes tracked his progress as he drove by. The next vacant space was two or three spots down the row.

After he'd parked, he turned off the ignition and reached across to retrieve the blazer he'd thrown over the passenger seat. As his hand closed over the fabric, he realized he was probably overdressed as it was.

He changed the motion he'd begun. He raised his chin, fingers working to loosen the knot of his tie.

As they did, his gaze shifted and found Cara standing outside the passenger-side door. The transformation in her appearance was so great he almost didn't recognize her.

Tonight she was wearing a red knit top, which exposed a lot of arm and throat and even some cleavage, and a pair of worn jeans. Her hair was loose and straight, silver-gilt under the string of lights that had been hung across the parking lot.

She put her hand on the outside handle, waiting for him to release the lock. When he did, she opened the door and began to slide into the other seat.

At the same time, Nick reached for his blazer, intending to toss it into the back and out of the way. His fingers collided with her cheekbone. She flinched, raising her hand to touch the spot they'd bumped.

"Sorry. I was reaching for my jacket."

She leaned forward, allowing him to lift the blazer off the seat and then pitch it into the rear. He turned back to find she was watching him.

The place on her cheek had begun to redden a little. He wondered what it would feel like to run his thumb over the mark he'd just made on that smooth, translucent skin.

It was an urge he was smart enough to resist. That aura of untouchability that surrounded her was so strong it was almost a shield. He wasn't arrogant enough to believe it was there for his benefit. That had been in place from the first time he'd seen her.

"I take it we aren't going inside," he said.

"Are you hungry?"

He hadn't been. Not until the aroma from the roasting pit had carried through the night air. Its fragrance provided a weird but not unpleasant undernote to the perfume she was wearing.

"I can wait," he said.

However she wanted to play this was fine by him. He'd already gotten further in this quest than he had dared to hope when he'd started.

"Don Crawford died of a heart attack," she said.

Assault number one on the theories he'd presented to her at her father's wake. It was nothing he hadn't expected.

"He was forty-one."

"High-stress job. Unhealthy lifestyle. Heredity."

"Murder." Nick's tone was as reasoned as hers. Only the word he'd chosen to add to her list hinted at sarcasm.

"If he *had* been murdered," she countered calmly, "don't you think the FBI would know?"

"That would depend on how closely they were looking at his death. A lot of drugs can mimic a coronary. The Bureau can probably screen for ninety percent of them. *If* they want to."

"If they'd had any reason to suspect foul play in Crawford's death, they would have. And before you ask, no, they didn't."

It was obvious that was the party line. And just as obvious that she had used her contacts within the Bureau to hear it. And that, of course, was why he needed her. The thing that would make her such a valuable ally.

Despite the way she looked, Cara Simonson was a certified computer geek. According to the information he'd uncovered, she always had been, following at a very young age in the footsteps of a neighbor boy, who had been a very talented programmer and hacker.

She had capitalized on those early experiences by earning a couple of degrees on her way to her current position with one of the nation's fastest growing information technology companies. And her firm's most recent contract, the big fat company-making government kind, had been to work on the ongoing upgrades of the FBI's computer systems.

Nick believed that made her his best shot at getting at the truth of whatever his father—and hers—had been involved in. Something that had also resulted in the death of an FBI special agent.

"They need a reason to suspect foul play?" he asked. "How about because Crawford died on the same day he was supposed to meet with my father. Who, strangely enough, committed suicide a couple of days after he'd agreed to that meeting. I don't know about you, but that's a little too much coincidence for me."

Her pupils had dilated slightly when he'd mentioned his father's suicide. Whatever she'd been told by the Bureau, it hadn't included that information.

"Coincidences happen."

Assault number two.

"Except I knew my dad. He wasn't somebody who spent his days looking at snapshots from 'Nam. He wasn't somebody who would drive fifty miles to meet a stranger for dinner. And he damn sure wasn't the kind of guy to eat his own gun."

He had kept his voice deliberately low, but emotion had crept in at the last. He swallowed hard, trying to control a fury he hadn't realized he felt.

"People change. Growing old can be difficult, especially if…" Mercifully, she let the sentence fade.

It didn't matter. Nick couldn't have denied any sin of neglect she might have chosen to use to fill that blank. He and his father had never been close, but especially not during the last few years.

Although Nick would have thought his dad would be more capable of putting a gun to someone else's head than to his own, when they'd called to tell him about his father, he hadn't been so adamant about rejecting suicide as the cause of death. Not then. If he were honest, he would have to admit his conviction that his dad hadn't killed himself had crystallized only *after* he'd started to put the other stuff together.

"He wasn't wearing his seat belt."

Because he had been thinking about his own father, it took too long to put that into context. And when he had—

"*Your* dad?"

She nodded, no longer looking at him but out through the windshield. To a casual observer, it would appear as if she were watching the crowd around the restaurant door. He doubted she was conscious of anything about the scene before her.

"He *always* put his belt on. Always. It was as natural to him as breathing. Something he didn't have to think about anymore."

Nick could have reminded her that with enough alcohol even automatic responses can be disrupted. If a seat belt was what she needed to convince her, however, he wasn't stupid enough to argue the point.

"Maybe if it were only that…" She paused, shaking her head slightly. Then she took a breath, pressing her lips together before she opened them again. "The police gave me the name of the place where they had the car towed. I went to see it. It was…"

Another hesitation, this one much longer than the first. Nick waited through it, trying not to rush her toward the conclusion he needed her to reach. At this point, if he tried to do that, it would only make her pull away.

"The seat was wrong. He always pushed it all the way back because he was so tall. It wasn't in that position. If it had been the other way around—pushed farther back than normal—I could believe that maybe they'd moved it while they were trying to get him out of the car, but this way…"

She shook her head again from side to side. Slowly. As if she were still considering the possibilities.

"It just doesn't make sense," she said finally.

"Unless someone else drove his car."

"Nobody did," she said quickly. "I asked. And then I did what you suggested. I talked to the cop who wrote up the report. To them it was obvious what had happened. They didn't question what they'd found. They just accepted it."

Like the Bureau had accepted Don Crawford's death.

"You don't."

"The owner of the junkyard gave me the things they found in the car. He thought they should be returned to my mother since the investigation's over."

Whatever the guy had given her, Nick realized, this was what had driven her to him. She wasn't the kind of person who would be satisfied with the evidence of the belt and the seat position. Those could be too easily explained away.

And that meant they had made a mistake. There had been nothing like that in the staging of his father's death. He had looked for it. Something out of place. Some slipup. Something they'd overlooked.

There had been nothing. If Don Crawford hadn't left

that message after his father died, Nick wouldn't be here. He would never have suspected what had really happened.

"What kind of things?" he asked, trying to contain his excitement. He couldn't prevent the surge of adrenaline that roared through his body, despite how certain he'd been before that he was right.

"My father may have been a drunk," Cara said, turning to face him again, "but he was a discriminating one."

"They used the wrong brand." He had deleted the second adjective before he could voice it, although it had certainly been in his head. He couldn't resist adding, almost triumphantly, "Son of a bitch."

"If my daddy had set out to tie one on, he would have done it with the same stuff he always drank. And that *wasn't* what was in the bottle they found in his car the night he died."

Chapter Four

"When I tried to get in touch with Crawford, I ended up at the main switchboard of the FBI. The agent assigned to take over Crawford's cases told me he'd had a heart attack on the same day he was supposed to meet my dad. That's when I started trying to identify the names on my father's list."

"And they were all first names?" Cara asked as she watched Nick take a long draw of the beer the waitress had just brought to their table.

The story he'd told had sounded almost dispassionate, even when he'd been speaking about his father's death. It had also been cogent and to the point, Cara admitted. No embellishments. No claim to understand more of what was going on than he could back up with evidence.

And there was enough of it so that she couldn't dismiss out of hand what he was saying—as bizarre as it sounded. Nick believed someone was killing the men whose names had been on his father's list. He also believed, but couldn't yet prove, that they were connected to something that had happened in Vietnam almost thirty-five years ago.

"I started with your father. For obvious reasons."

Of course. Hiram Simonson would be a lot easier to locate than John Doe.

"How did you find him? Even with his first name—"

"Battalion records."

"I'm surprised the army gave you access."

He didn't answer immediately, taking another swallow of his beer to cover the delay. For the first time she had the feeling that he was deciding what to tell her.

"They're probably available to the public. Somewhere. I didn't want to jump through whatever bureaucratic hoops getting to them would require, so I called in a favor."

"From someone in the Pentagon, I presume?"

There was another pause, one that lengthened almost to discomfort before he said, "From a friend."

Her instinct was right. Whatever Nick Morelli had done, whatever strings he'd pulled, he didn't intend to talk about them. Obviously, he was protecting whomever—probably someone in the Department of the Army—he'd called that favor in from.

Which was all right with her. She felt the same way about the agent she'd contacted this afternoon. Burke Raymond was someone she'd met socially rather than during the course of the project her company was working on. For some reason that had made it easier to call him to inquire about Crawford.

"I asked my source for a listing of people in my father's battalion during his dates of service. He faxed me the names and old addresses from the database. Your father's name was on the list. Luckily he was still living in the same area as was shown on his service records. I located him in the phone directory."

Her father had grown up here. After the war, he'd come home, gone to law school, and eventually joined her grandfather's practice. Despite his drinking, he had been a very successful attorney. Under his leadership the firm had grown to regional prominence after handling several high profile government cases.

"By the time I got his location, however, he'd been dead twenty-four hours."

She'd had no idea it had been so close. Twenty-four hours. One day.

"I'm sorry I wasn't quicker," Nick added softly.

She shook her head, stunned by the revelation. "Then *your* father's death…" She hesitated, trying to calculate the passage of time.

"My father died six days ago. I didn't know anything about any of this until after his funeral. Maybe if I'd gone through the stuff at his house before—"

"Don't," she ordered.

He was no more responsible for her father's death than for the death of his own. And she had finally realized that his grief was as new as hers. Adding the burden of guilt to it wouldn't bring either of their fathers back. The only thing they could do now…

"What about the others?" she asked. "The names on your dad's list. Did you find them, too?"

Without answering, he reached into the breast pocket of his shirt and drew out a folded sheet of paper. He opened it with his thumb, holding it out to her across the table.

The names had been printed in broad black strokes. Without looking at the sheet, Nick repeated the remaining ones aloud as she read them silently.

"Scottie, John, Buddy and The Shark. The last is obviously a nickname. Scottie may be, as well. There was no Scott listed during the time frame. Neither as a first or a last name."

The implications of this were only now beginning to register. Two of the men on the list she held were dead, along with an FBI agent who'd had contact with at least one of them. And if Nick was right, the rest were targets.

"We need to find out what Crawford was working on," he said.

We. It was the first time he had used the plural pronoun, although she realized that she had already been thinking in those terms.

Despite that, she was unsure what kind of commitment she was being asked to make. Trying to find out what Crawford had been working on wasn't the same kind of casual query she'd made to the agent she'd contacted this afternoon.

And whatever was going on seemed to be moving at breakneck speed. If Nick was right, three people had already been murdered in less than a week. Some of the others may have been, as well.

They were way behind the curve. And no matter what they did, it was too late for his father or for hers.

For her, however, there was another consideration. Something guaranteed to draw her into becoming involved with Nick Morelli's quest. A quietly whispered confession.

I'd give almost anything…

How important would it be for her mother to know that *nothing* had happened the day her father died? To understand that whatever had torn their lives apart hadn't been an action he'd initiated, but something that had been done *to* him. Something evil that had reached into their happiness from the outside and snatched it away.

"He ever talk about 'Nam?"

Nick's question brought her abruptly back to the present. She didn't really know how to answer it. Her mother had talked *at* her dad about the war. She couldn't ever remember him answering, no matter what the provocation.

"My mother always thought that's where his problems started."

"The alcoholism?"

She nodded, remembering a time when she hadn't had a name for it. Remembering the arguments and the long silences. Remembering her mother waiting by the phone and remembering being told to be quiet the following morning when she played.

"He never said much about what happened to him there. I always thought that was the norm—not wanting to talk about it. It didn't seem to me that he was being particularly secretive. Just that the experience was something he'd rather forget."

"My dad refused to talk about it. He'd walk away if anyone did. And he was the toughest SOB I've ever met."

"He stayed in after the war?"

"Twenty years. Whatever happened, it didn't make him hate the Army. And he didn't object when I wanted to enlist."

"Did you?"

"At eighteen. I think I wanted to prove I was as tough as he was."

Tall, dark and dangerous. She had known that from the moment he'd taken her arm at the wake and said, *I think your father was murdered.*

"Are you career military?" she asked.

"I didn't last that long."

There was something in his voice that warned her not to press him. She couldn't believe it was because he'd quit or failed to qualify. But whatever the reason, it was unlikely he would share it with her tonight.

"Smells good," he said as the waitress set their plates down in front of them.

The change in subject didn't surprise her. Nick didn't seem comfortable when the focus was on him.

And there was no reason for this to get personal. They were strangers who had been thrust together because of something neither of them wanted to be involved in. He was right to guard his privacy. She intended to guard hers.

She leaned forward, closing her eyes and breathing in the aroma of the barbecue. Both smoky-sweet and sharp, the smell unexpectedly made her mouth water.

She couldn't remember the last time she'd eaten. Maybe the few bites of the sandwich she'd shared with her mother last night. She hadn't been hungry since she'd arrived, and today there had been too much to do to think about food.

She opened her eyes and found Nick watching her. In this light his eyes were more brown than black. Yesterday they had seemed as dark as his hair.

"I hope you aren't the kind of woman who'll take one bite of that and say you're full," he said, picking up his own heavily laden sandwich.

There was a movement at one corner of his mouth. Almost a tilt. So subtle that if she hadn't been watching him, she would have missed it.

And as she picked up her sandwich, she had to admit that she really would have hated that.

WHEN THEY CAME OUT of the restaurant, the crowd around the door had disappeared, although there were still plenty of cars in the parking lot. After the chill of the air conditioner inside, Cara welcomed the comparative warmth of the early fall air over her bare arms.

As she began to descend the three steps leading down from the low porch, Nick's fingers cupped under her elbow. It was an impersonal gesture, the kind of old-fashioned politeness that still lingered in the South. She might have been more surprised had he *not* offered that support.

As soon as they were on the asphalt, he removed his hand, but she was conscious of the place where he'd touched her, almost as if she could still feel the warmth of his fingers against her skin.

It was definitely a man's hand. Strong. Callused. The fingertips a little rough.

"There's not much more we can do tonight," he said. "I'm supposed to touch base with my source tomorrow. He's still trying to make some matches with those names."

"My mother might remember something. Maybe one of the nicknames. Or maybe just the name of someone Daddy was close to there. Maybe someone who would know who those people are. It's worth a shot."

"Anything that can get us closer is worth a shot."

He had been living with the urgency of this longer than she had. Even as they'd talked tonight, someone else, someone like her father or his, someone long past that terrible jungle war, was in danger. And until they discovered the identities of those four men, there wasn't a damn thing they could do about it.

Nick placed his hand under her elbow again as they

approached the end of the sidewalk. He checked for oncoming traffic off the access road before he stepped forward, carrying her with him. He didn't release her as they began to walk across to her mother's car.

"Could you ask whoever you called today about Crawford? There's got to be a way to find out what he was working on."

It was the second time he'd hinted at the importance of that information. Was it possible he knew about the project and thought she could access the FBI's files? If so, he obviously didn't have any idea about the kind of security breach that would be.

"Why don't we just lay it out for them?" she suggested. "Tell the Bureau what we think is going on. If you're right about Crawford—"

The squeal of tires against asphalt caused her to break off the sentence. Their heads turned in unison in the direction of the sound even as their forward progress slowed.

A car screamed around the back corner of the restaurant, making the turn on two wheels. Its headlights were off, but the dangling bulbs on the string above their heads were reflected in its finish as it roared toward them.

Nick reacted more quickly than she did. Before her brain could command her feet to move, he put his hand against the small of her back and shoved as hard as he could.

She staggered a couple of steps, trying desperately to keep from falling. Just as she thought she might regain her balance, Nick's hand hit her between the shoulders, knocking her forward to slam into the hood of the Mercedes. Somehow she got her arms up in time to keep from landing facedown on top of it.

Without slowing, the car careered out of the lot

and fishtailed onto the access road. Cara lifted her head in time to watch its taillights blend into the flow of traffic on the interstate.

The entire incident had taken only seconds. If not for the stench of burned rubber, it would have been hard to believe it had really happened.

She turned and found Nick on his hands and knees at the front of her mother's car. He was holding his body upright with his right arm. The elbow was locked, his palm flat against the pavement. His other arm was pressed against his side. He had managed to push her out of harm's way, but clearly he hadn't escaped unscathed.

She dropped down beside him, unthinkingly putting her arm across his hunched shoulders. The muscles in his back, even covered by the oxford cloth shirt he wore, were hard and warm beneath her bare skin. Despite their obvious strength, a small vibration ran through his body periodically, as if he were fighting a chill.

She leaned forward, trying to see his face, but all that was visible was his profile. His eyes were closed, his lips pressed together so tightly they were bloodless.

"Are you all right?"

He opened his eyes in response and began to straighten in stages. During the last one, he lifted the hand he was propping on off the pavement. As he came upright, still on his knees, some inarticulate sound—a cross between a sigh and a groan—slipped from between his lips.

His eyes searched the access road behind her before they returned to hers. "Tag number?"

It had happened so fast she hadn't had time to think

about that. She couldn't even be certain about the color of the car. Dark. Navy or black or that deep forest-green that was so popular right now.

"I'm sorry."

She was. The one thing she should have done automatically, and she hadn't even thought about it.

"Doesn't matter. Probably stolen."

Nick seemed to be rationing his words. His mouth was open, and he was breathing through it, each breath slow and carefully shallow.

"You want me to call the police?" she asked.

"You get a description of the driver?"

She shook her head. "It all happened so fast. I didn't have time to react. Thank you for—"

She was about to say "for saving my life." Even though that was obviously what he had done, the words seemed almost bizarre. Melodramatic. People didn't really say things like that. Not in real life.

"I'd say this particular method needs more work," Nick said, just as if he hadn't heard what she was trying to say.

"This...method?"

"They should stick to staged suicides. Or heart attacks. Less public and apparently a hell of a lot more efficient. After all...*we* survived."

Chapter Five

"I still think you should go to the emergency room. There's always the possibility that you have—"

"A couple of bruised ribs."

Nick managed to get the words out with the same economy of breath he'd displayed since she'd knelt beside him on the pavement outside the restaurant. She knew he was in a lot of pain but, exasperatingly, he had refused to even consider medical treatment.

Since he wouldn't go to the hospital, taking him home with her had seemed the next best solution. Far better than letting him go back to his motel room alone.

She hadn't told him that, of course. Despite his injuries, the only way she had managed to get him here was to offer her mother's help in identifying the men on his father's list.

He was negotiating the front steps of her parents' house by taking them slowly and using the banister. She moved ahead of him to insert her key into the front door, but before she could turn it in the lock, the door opened. Her mother was dressed in her robe, but she had obviously not yet gone to bed.

"I thought I heard the car."

Her eyes focused on the man who was pulling himself up her front steps. Rushing forward, she put her narrow shoulder under Nick's free arm.

Her mother's action didn't surprise Cara. Nick's willingness to accept her help did, however. And it made her feel guilty that she hadn't dared to offer her own.

It was typical that her mother didn't ask any questions. She never had. She had always jumped right in, whether it was at the ballpark or Girl Scout camp, doing what needed to be done without waiting for explanations. After working for over twenty-five years as an RN, that had been as natural to her as breathing. It still was.

"Bathroom," she ordered as she helped Nick through the door Cara held open.

Cara laid her purse on the hall credenza and trailed the two of them down the hall. Her mother flicked on the bathroom light and then stepped aside to allow Nick to go through the narrow door. She entered after him, leaving Cara to stand in the hallway.

"I take it we aren't calling the authorities about whatever happened," her mother said.

"Nor going to the hospital," Cara said.

Nick had ignored the question, propping one hip on the countertop. He sat slightly hunched forward, his arms crossed over his stomach.

"How about you? Are you hurt?" her mother asked, throwing a glance at Cara over her shoulder.

She would probably be sore tomorrow, especially the wrist she'd used to break her fall when Nick had thrown her against the hood of the car. Other than that…

"I'm fine," she said. "He says it's bruised ribs, but he seems to be in a lot of pain."

"Ribs hurt like hell, whether they're bruised or broken," her mother said. "And that's very hard to determine without X rays."

The last had obviously been addressed to Nick as she began to unfasten the buttons on his shirt. Again to Cara's surprise, he didn't object, closing his eyes and leaning back against the mirror behind him. His skin looked gray beneath its tan.

"I need my good scissors. They're on the sewing machine in the guest bedroom." Her mother had finished with the buttons and was carefully easing the dress shirt off over Nick's shoulder.

"Scissors?"

"To cut off this undershirt. No sense in making him go through the agony of taking it off over his head. Your father's got plenty."

As soon as the unthinking reference to her husband came out of her mouth, her mother turned to look at Cara. Both pain at the sudden memory of their loss and an apology for the reminder were in her eyes.

For Cara, the mention of her father brought back all the things Nick had told her tonight. She knew that now wasn't the time to share them with her mother. That would have to come after Nick had been taken care of.

She shook her head, trying to let her mom know that she understood. It was hard for her to remember that her daddy was gone. For her mother, whose life had revolved around him for so long—

"Go on." Her mother had already refocused her attention on her patient.

Even if she couldn't help them with the names, Cara thought, even if Nick's theory was eventually proved to be wrong, her mother had needed this.

Someone to take care of. Something to keep the grief at bay if only for a little while.

"And lock the front door," Nick ordered without opening his eyes.

Of course. How stupid that she hadn't done that already, Cara thought, heading down the hallway to obey the instructions she'd been given. If Nick was right about what was going on, someone had tried to kill them tonight.

And they would try again, she realized, her blood running cold. After all, they had nothing to lose by adding to the building body count.

BY THE TIME she returned with the scissors, her mother had succeeded in peeling off Nick's dress shirt and pulling his T-shirt out of the waistband of his trousers. She used her sewing shears to slit the side of the undershirt and along the underarm sleeve. Even before she completed the job, cutting across the shoulder to the neckband and slipping the garment off Nick's other arm, the damage was visible.

The skin where the car had struck him was discolored, the rapidly darkening bruise running from about halfway down his side to disappear under the waistband of his trousers. Despite its vividness, the injury hadn't been the first thing that had drawn Cara's eyes.

Under the bronzed skin, Nick's arms and shoulders were corded with muscle. Not the overdeveloped kind a weight lifter might have, but the long, firm muscles hard physical activity built. His pecs were particularly well defined. Then his chest narrowed to what was often referred to as a washboard set of abs. The arrow of dark hair that centered those disappeared into the top of his waistband, just like the discoloration.

Cara would have said she wasn't the kind of woman who could be turned on by the sight of a man's bare chest—especially that of a stranger. There was no denying, however, that looking at Nick, her mouth had unaccountably gone dry.

Trying to block the image of that blatantly masculine body, she concentrated on watching her mother's experienced fingers, which were carefully examining his injury. As Miriam touched the area where the bruising started, Nick flinched, and then quickly controlled any other reaction.

"If you're going to crack ribs," her mother said, continuing to run her fingers over the area, "these are the best. Any lower and you risk damage to the spleen. Any higher and—" The words were abruptly cut off as Nick flinched again.

"Then they are broken?" Cara asked.

Nick's eyes were still closed, so thankfully he was unaware of the number of times Cara had glanced at his face from under her lashes while ostensibly watching her mother's evaluation.

"It's really impossible to tell without X rays," her mom said, "but...I can't feel any lumps or hear anything that makes me think so. Any pain in your shoulder?"

"My shoulder?"

"If there were damages to your spleen, the bleeding might cause that."

"No," Nick said shortly.

"Then let's see about your hip."

Not only his side, then, Cara realized. If his leg was also damaged, that would explain the trouble Nick had had coming up the steps.

"It's just bruised," he said, as obstinate about that as he'd been about everything else.

"I still think you should get everything X-rayed. It's the only way to tell how much—"

"No X rays. No hospital," Nick interrupted. "It's you or nobody."

There was probably nothing he could have said that would appeal to her mother more than that. She was the ultimate caretaker. Maybe that's why she'd put up with her husband's drinking as long as she had. And just when it seemed that their lives had finally settled down into a true happiness—

"Then you're going to have to let me see the hip, too," her mother said.

There was a tense moment of silence. Cara found herself holding her breath through it, but in the end, Nick gave in to the inevitable.

He began to ease up off the counter, grimacing as he put weight on the damaged leg. For all his protestations, it was obvious that he was hurting badly. If he hadn't thrown her out of the way…

"We'll need your help, dear," her mother said. "Put his arm over your shoulder."

As she moved into the position she'd been directed to take, Cara was surrounded by the same pleasant fragrance she'd notice when she'd been sitting in Nick's car. Aftershave maybe. Or soap. Shampoo. Something subtle, in any case. Clean, totally masculine, and incredibly appealing.

For a fraction of a second, she actually wondered if her mom might be trying to play matchmaker, despite the situation. That suspicion was destroyed when her mother began undoing the buckle of the belt holding up Nick's trousers, reminding Cara of the discoloration that had extended down his side.

No matter how attracted Cara was to Nick

Morelli, and it was pretty ridiculous at this point to try to deny she was, her mother was only doing what she had always done. What she had been trained to do. Taking care of someone who needed her help.

Mouth again dry, Cara lifted Nick's right arm and put it over her shoulders. As she did, she realized that his height was probably no more than three or four inches above her own five foot seven. Somehow, from the moment she'd met him, he had seemed much taller.

Awkwardly, she put her arm around his back, feeling the same hard muscles there that had been visible on his chest. He leaned against her as her mother began to pull the top of his pants and his briefs down far enough to look at the injured hip.

From her position on Nick's other side, Cara couldn't see the damage. And given her reactions up to this point to seeing him partially undressed, that was probably a blessing.

"I think you're right," her mom said after a few minutes of examination. "That's not to say it won't be sore, but I don't think this is anything more than bruising. The ribs are the more serious injury."

"Can you wrap them?" Nick asked.

"Only if you want pneumonia."

"I don't understand."

"If they *are* broken, then binding them might make them feel marginally better, but it will also restrict your breathing. And you've got to breathe deeply to avoid fluid buildup."

"Are you saying there's nothing you can do?" Cara asked.

"Actually, there isn't much anyone would do. A doctor would give you painkillers and advise rest. And avoiding any movement that puts a strain on them until they heal, of course."

It didn't sound like a regimen that would fit with Nick's plans to track down whoever had killed his father. And who had, in all probability, murdered her dad, as well.

Tonight's attack had made her far more willing to buy into what had at first sounded like some insane conspiracy theory. Now…

"Would wrapping them give me more mobility?"

At Nick's question, Cara's eyes came up to find his still focused on her mother's face. The overhead light revealed a sheen of perspiration on his upper lip, despite the five-o'clock shadow that darkened his lean cheeks.

"Maybe," her mother acknowledged, "but you won't find a health-care professional who would do that. It isn't safe."

"Safety isn't my primary concern right now."

"But—"

For the first time, he turned his head to look down into Cara's eyes. "If I'd gotten here twenty-four hours earlier, your father might still be alive. I don't have time to *rest*." The final word received a bitter emphasis.

"What does that mean? If you'd gotten here earlier, Hi might be alive? What the hell are you talking about?" Her mother's voice had grown increasingly agitated with each question.

"Mom—"

"I didn't ask you, Cara. I asked him. What does that mean? What you just said?"

"I don't think your husband got drunk and drove his car into a tree."

Her mom's head tilted slightly as if she were processing that information. The faded blue eyes focused briefly on Cara's face before they returned to Nick.

"What *do* you think?" she asked softly.

"I think somebody murdered him, Mrs. Simonson, and set it up to look like an accident. And unless we stop them, I think they're going to do it again."

Chapter Six

"It all sounds…"

"Unbelievable," Cara finished when her mother hesitated.

Once Nick had dropped that bombshell, they had really had no choice but to lay out his theory for Miriam, although she had insisted on giving him something for pain before she'd heard it. Then she had listened with the same concentration with which she approached anything new she was trying to comprehend.

"You *do* understand that Nick doesn't have absolute proof of this," Cara warned. "It's just that the combination of circumstances—".

"If it isn't true, then why would someone try to run the two of you down?"

She should have known her mother would latch on to this theory as fact. After all, it was a more acceptable explanation for her father's death. She would far rather believe in Nick's conspiracy than in the scenario the police had outlined. And Cara had to admit that the case he'd laid out had been convincing.

"Maybe whoever was driving that car tonight was drunk. Or maybe one had nothing to do with the other. Either with Daddy's death or Nick's father's suicide."

"Or with Special Agent Crawford's convenient heart attack," Nick added, his tone mocking.

"And the hit-and-run attempt tonight was just *another* coincidence?" her mother asked. "Is that what you're suggesting."

"I'm just saying that—"

She stopped because the skepticism in the two pairs of eyes focused on her face made any other caveats ridiculous. There was a point at which a reasonable person stopped believing in happenstance. It was obvious that both her mother and Nick had already reached it.

She wasn't sure why the possibility her father had been murdered was so hard for her to accept. Maybe because things like that didn't happen in her carefully controlled world.

She had a feeling they did in Nick's. Although he had shared very little about his background, other than mentioning that he'd been in the army, she suspected he was exactly what she had thought from the first time she'd seen him. Dark and very dangerous.

As for her mother, she would be willing to believe anything that relieved the guilt she'd been feeling. And reading between the lines, Cara thought there was probably an element of guilt involved in Nick's reaction to the death of his father. If it hadn't been for the death of the FBI agent and what had happened tonight—

Those added up to too many coincidences, even for someone like her. She took a breath before she completed the sentence she'd begun.

"It's hard to believe someone would deliberately set out to murder six innocent people."

"And you think all this has something to do with Vietnam?"

Her mother's attention had quickly returned to Nick. He was sitting in one of the dining room chairs, waiting for the painkiller she had given him to take effect. He still held his arm closely against his side, as if supporting his ribs, which indicated to Cara that the medication hadn't yet kicked in.

At least he had put his shirt back on. Although he hadn't bothered doing up all the buttons, thankfully he'd refastened enough of them that the trail of dark hair across that taut, tanned stomach was hidden.

"That appears to be the connection between them. At least it's the most obvious one. Did your husband ever mention my father, Mrs. Simonson? His name was Vincent. Vince Morelli."

"Call me Miriam, please." She thought about what he'd asked, pursing her lips as she did, before she shook her head. "I don't think so. Not that I can remember."

"Did he talk much about 'Nam?"

"Hardly ever. He didn't even watch movies about it. Cara, you remember how he was."

"Did he mention anything to you about something that might have happened there that…" Nick hesitated, searching for an appropriate phrasing.

"That might get him killed?" her mother asked bluntly. "I'd certainly remember *that*. There was never anything like that. Actually, he didn't say much about his time in the service at all. He was drafted. He went to Vietnam like thousands of other kids, and then he came home. It was just something that had happened to him. He didn't like it, of course—being away from home and all—but it didn't seem like that big a deal to him one way or the other. Not as far as I could tell."

"That list of names Nick's father made. I told him

that you should look at it," Cara said. "Maybe you'll recognize one of them."

It was the first time she had called him Nick aloud, although she had been thinking of him that way for several hours. She was also aware that he hadn't yet said her name, nothing other than Ms. Simonson, which was how he'd addressed her at the wake.

Given the fact that he had almost certainly saved her life tonight, it seemed that by now they should have moved on to something less formal. And she had a feeling that it would be up to her to make that change in their relationship. A change she was more than willing to have happen.

"I can't remember your dad talking about *anyone* over there by name, but then it's been more than thirty years. I'll be glad to take a look if you want."

Nick had already pulled the page that had been torn from his father's notepad out of the pocket of his shirt. He held it across the table, just as he'd done at the restaurant tonight.

Her mother opened it, lips pursing again as she studied the names. "Doesn't tell you much, does it? These could belong to anybody."

"Shark is obviously a nickname. You ever remember your husband referring to someone as Shark or The Shark?"

Again a slow negative movement of her head as she continued to study the list.

"How about Scottie?" Nick asked patiently.

"Someone who liked *Star Trek*, maybe? If that was even on back then. You know. Mr. Scott. The engineer. That's who *I* think of when I hear Scottie."

"Mom."

Cara's tone sounded chiding, and she hadn't really

meant it to, but this was getting them nowhere. She wondered if Nick was as frustrated by her mother's lack of information as she was.

Maybe she'd been too hopeful when they started this. After all, as her mother kept reminding them, all that had taken place a very long time ago.

"I don't think your daddy *talked* about the people he knew over there," Miriam said. "If he did, I've forgotten any of the names he might have mentioned."

"I have the list of everyone who was in the battalion around the time my father was in country. It's in my briefcase in the car. Maybe if you could look at it, one of the names might trigger something."

"Of course I'll look at it, but…it really has been a long time," Miriam said apologetically.

"I'll go out and get it," Cara offered.

"Not alone," Nick said.

He started to rise, but seemed to stagger forward a little, righting himself by putting one hand flat on the table. As he straightened, he made a sound low in his throat.

Cara realized belatedly that noise had been in response to the pain of moving. Despite the slight glaze in his eyes, the medication had obviously not dulled the effects of tonight's hit-and-run.

"We can do it in the morning," she said quickly. "You said there were over seven hundred names. I doubt that Mom is up to going over all of them tonight."

"There were that many people in Hi's unit?" her mother asked.

"I didn't want to narrow it down too far and risk eliminating someone we should be considering," Nick said. "I asked for the list of the battalion broken down by companies. We can start with your husband's company, but we can't know for sure that all of those names—" he nodded toward his father's handwritten list that was still lying in the middle of the table "—will be there."

"Then there're too many to try to contact them individually and warn them," Miriam said.

Cara had a quick mental image of the three of them calling hundreds of strangers with the message that someone might be trying to kill them. She could imagine the reactions.

Thankfully, Nick treated her mother's comment with a more serious consideration. "Far too many. Even if we had access to their current addresses. And we don't. It took me several hours to track down your husband, and he was still living in the same area."

"And he wasn't named Smith or Jones," Miriam said, obviously getting the point.

"Or Buddy or John," Cara added softly.

Again Nick's eyes focused on her face. She could read the frustration within them.

"We probably need to get the list and at least let your mom take a look at it. With the speed at which things are unfolding, we really can't afford to wait until morning. If they figure this out before we do, then someone else will die."

"If *they* figure it out? I don't understand," Cara said.

"I don't think they know who the people on my father's list are any more than we do. Not judging by the time that lapsed between the death of my father and yours."

"I don't understand," Miriam said.

"If they saw my father's list the day they killed

him, then it took them about the same amount of time to identify and find the next name on the list as it took me."

"You had access through your sources to the list from the Department of the Army. Are you saying they may have that same information?"

"It would seem that way."

"And you're also assuming that they didn't make my father their *last* target. That they haven't already taken care of the others."

"I am assuming that. If you didn't have anything to go on but the names on that list—" he nodded toward the notepaper "—which would you try to find first?"

Hiram, of course. Just as Nick had.

"You're making a lot of assumptions," she said, thinking about what he was suggesting.

"I prefer the term educated guesses," he corrected with a touch of amusement in his voice. "It just seemed to make sense to me."

"Then they aren't so far ahead of us. Not if they're figuring it out as they go along, just as we are."

"They were twenty-four hours ahead of me in getting to your father. If they'd been only fifteen minutes ahead of me, I couldn't have stopped them."

He was right. If Nick's theory was correct, he had discovered her father's identity more quickly than whoever had killed him, but they had still had enough of a head start that it had all been over before Nick arrived.

Which meant that even now, even as they sat here talking, someone was stalking another of the unsuspecting men on the list Nick's father had jotted down before someone crammed his service revolver into his mouth and pulled the trigger.

"You stay here," she said. "Mom can stand in the

front door and watch me. Nobody's going to try anything else tonight."

"That's probably what Don Crawford thought," Nick said, pushing away from the table.

Despite the effects of the pain pills and the glancing blow the car had struck him, he started limping toward the front of the house. Brows raised, Cara met her mother's eyes before she gave up and followed him.

"YOU CAN'T REMEMBER *anyone?*" Cara prodded.

Her mother's brow wrinkled as if to indicate she was really trying, but at the same time she shook her head. "There are so many of them. I just… I'm sorry, but none of these look familiar. Even if your father did mention someone, that would have been years ago. Or while he was still in Vietnam. I'm not sure I'd remember the name after all this time."

"What about his letters?" Nick had picked up on the significance of the phrase "while he was in Vietnam." Given the difficulty of telephoning for most of the frontline troops during that war, the most likely place for such a mention to have occurred would have been in written correspondence.

"You still have them," Cara said, feeling a surge of excitement.

Her mother had always kept the letters she and her father had exchanged in a suitcase in the top of the hall closet. The bag, white with large black flowers, was obviously a product of the '60s.

"We can look at them, of course, but I doubt you'll find anything of value. Hi wasn't much for talking about what was going on there. Those letters contain mostly personal things. Answering what I wrote to him about. Talking about friends here and what they were doing. I mean, he may have mentioned *someone* from his unit…" She shook her head again.

"It's worth a chance," Nick said, looking straight at Cara for the first time since they'd sat back down at the table.

He had already been halfway across the lawn when she had reached the front door. Although she could have waited for him there, she had chosen to follow him out to his car instead. She'd arrived in time to watch him remove a pistol from the briefcase he'd come out to retrieve and stick it into the waistband of his trousers.

He had turned, meeting her eyes, but neither of them had made any comment about the gun. It was very tangible evidence, however, of how different Nick Morelli was from the men she had known. The fact that he carried a weapon in his briefcase reinforced the conclusions she had already drawn about him.

"I know where those letters are," Cara said. "I can go through them tonight, looking for names. That won't take me as long as actually reading them. And I won't do that, Mom, I promise."

"There's nothing there I'd care about you seeing. Besides, maybe your dad did make reference to whatever this is Nick thinks happened. You won't see it if you're just looking for names. We better divide them. The reading will go faster that way. And from what Nick has said—"

Miriam stopped abruptly, but the reminder was just as powerful as if she'd completed it. This was a race against time, pure and simple, with the lives of the rest of those men on his father's list as the stakes.

Chapter Seven

Cara was reading, her forehead propped on one hand, fingers threaded through her hair. The chandelier over the kitchen table where she sat highlighted its fairness.

Nick watched a moment from the doorway, feeling like a voyeur, but unable to pull his eyes away. Her parents' letters were spread out on the table in front of her, arranged in neat lines that he would bet corresponded to the months during that year her father had spent in Vietnam.

When she finished the one she'd been reading, she picked up the pages and began to fold them to reinsert into the envelope. At some point in the process, she became aware he was watching her.

As her eyes locked with his, Nick didn't have to ask if she'd found anything. The frustration in her face spoke volumes.

"She was right," she said with a trace of bitterness. "Whatever else he might have been, my father was a terrible correspondent. No names. And damn few incidents. It's like he didn't want to talk about what was going on over there."

Nick nodded without bothering to state the obvious. Most of the people who had served in that war probably felt the same way, given the way it had been politicized in this country. Men like his father and Hi Simonson came home and never told anyone about the impact the months they'd spent in Southeast Asia had had on their lives.

"How about the company list? Did your mom recognize any of the names?"

Despite her pledge to help Cara go through the letters, Miriam had at some point left her to finish the task alone. Nick couldn't blame her for not wanting to read her husband's writing only a few of days after his murder. Remembering how he'd felt going through his father's papers, he could imagine how difficult this had been for Cara, as well.

"She probably was right about that, too. He probably *didn't* mention any of those people to her. At least she didn't recognize anyone."

Which left the search exactly where they had been last night. No closer to identifying any of the remaining names on his father's list.

The only thing that had changed was that now Nick was also being hunted, something he hadn't expected, at least not this quickly. And because Cara had agreed to meet with him, he was afraid that he had also put her in the line of fire.

"There's coffee," she offered.

That's probably what had attracted him to the kitchen, Nick realized. He could smell it now, the aroma always better than the taste or even the caffeine kick it provided. Not that he couldn't use the latter this morning.

The medication Miriam had given him had worn off about an hour ago. Although he was still convinced that he was battered rather than broken, the combination of discomfort and the sense of time slipping away had driven him to drag his aching body out of bed at first light. In the absolute silence of the house, somehow he had ended up here.

"Thanks," he said.

He began to cross the room, trying not to favor the leg that had taken the brunt of the impact with the car's fender last night. Obviously he wasn't too successful because Cara's command stopped him halfway to the coffeemaker.

"Sit down. I'll get it."

For once in his life, Nick controlled the automatic refusal of assistance. For one thing, his hip and side hurt like hell. For another, he was finding the sight of Cara Simonson's long, tanned legs, revealed below the hem of the thigh-length nightshirt she wore, as jolting as he had anticipated her coffee would be.

He obediently changed course as Cara crossed to the coffeemaker. He eased down into one of the wooden kitchen chairs, looking up in time to watch her stretch to reach a mug in one of the top cabinets. He quickly lowered his eyes to the stacks of letters, concentrating on them rather than the additional inch or two of thigh that motion had exposed.

He'd been right about the sorting process. Even reading upside down, he could tell from the postmarks that each row represented a single month.

After a moment Cara set a steaming mug down in front of him, but she didn't resume her seat across the table. She stood beside him instead, forcing him to turn his head to meet her eyes.

"It seems we've reached a dead end with any help my mom or these letters might give us, so now what?"

Nick didn't comment on the unintended irony in her

word choice. "If we can't identify any of the other names on the list, we'll have to try some other approach."

Although she wasn't as close as she'd been last night when she had lifted his arm over her shoulders, he was very much aware of her as a woman. A highly desirable woman.

And he didn't have time for that kind of distraction right now. Four lives depended on how quickly he could figure out what was going on.

"Like what?" she asked.

He hesitated, certain from just the few hours he'd known her that she was going to resist what he was about to say. Other than trying to locate every John on the battalion list until he found the right one, however, he didn't know what else to suggest.

"We go in from the government side. We try to find out what Crawford was working on."

"How do you intend—"

There was nothing wrong with her intellect, Nick acknowledged as she realized what he was suggesting. Whether she would be willing to do what he wanted was an entirely different issue.

"No," she said.

"The lives of four men, men just like your father— and mine," he added almost reluctantly, "are at stake."

"I can't just go into the Bureau's system and start looking around, if that's really what you're suggesting. If Crawford was murdered, then whatever was in his case files becomes evidence. I could go to jail for tampering with it. I could probably go to jail in any case because that kind of activity is not only illegal, it's also highly unethical for someone in my position. Maybe that doesn't mean anything to you—"

She stopped abruptly, closing her lips as if to keep the rest of what she obviously considered an insult from slipping out. Considering the things he'd done for the agency through the years, his sense of right and wrong was probably far more pragmatic than most people's. Obviously more than hers.

"I'm sorry," she said. "I didn't mean that personally. I have no way of knowing how you would feel about doing something unethical."

"That it isn't life and death," Nick said.

The impact of that reminder was reflected in her eyes. She didn't answer right away. He gave her credit for at least being willing to think about what he was asking.

"Not only are there national security issues and the possibility of criminal charges," she said finally, "there are also issues for my employer, as well."

"Any that are worth a man's life?"

"If it ever came to light that I'd done something like that, we would lose the contract. If that happened, a lot of innocent people would lose their jobs. Stockholders would lose their investments. *And* I'd go to jail."

"Given what's been going on, you wouldn't go to jail. Not once we got to the bottom of this."

"And if we don't get to the bottom of it? Or if Crawford wasn't working on anything having to do with Vietnam? If his death really was a heart attack? If their meeting wasn't involved in your father's death? What then?"

"If you don't think you can to do it without getting caught, maybe there's someone else in your company who can."

"You think I'm going to approach one of my colleagues and ask them to violate the security of the FBI's system? You've lost your mind."

He said nothing, lifting the cup of coffee she'd brought him to his lips. After a moment she walked around the table and resumed her seat, making a show of replacing the letter she'd returned to its envelope in the correct stack.

Her mouth still tight, she picked up her own mug. Over the rim, her eyes met his.

"And I'm as good as anyone there," she said challengingly.

Nick didn't press his point, letting the silence build. He knew she would continue to think about what he'd asked and most of all about the validity of his argument.

If all else failed, he'd appeal to Griff. Maybe someone at the CIA could access those files, legally or not. At least there wouldn't be any talk of ethics from them.

"Sorry I flaked out on you last night."

Nick turned to find Miriam standing in the doorway from where he'd watched Cara only a few minutes ago. Her navy silk robe was far more modest than her daughter's nightshirt. She met his eyes briefly, an acknowledgement of his presence, before she looked at Cara.

"Did you find anything useful?"

Cara shook her head, her eyes still reflecting her anger over Nick's suggestion. To hide that from her mother, she looked down into her coffee. After a few seconds, she put both hands around the mug as if to warm them, but she didn't lift it again.

"I've been thinking about the names on your list," Miriam went on as she walked over to the coffeepot.

Thankfully she didn't seem aware of the tension that had been thick in the room before she'd entered.

"You've thought of something?" Nick prodded carefully.

"I don't know. It's just…you've been trying to fit Scottie to something. Thinking it might be a nickname for someone named Scott. What if it's a nickname for someone who's Scottish instead."

"Scots," Cara corrected. Despite her anger, she looked at Nick. "It's possible."

"But the name on the list is spelled with two *t*'s," Nick reminded her.

"Was your dad that good a speller?" Cara asked. "Or would he have been concerned with the proper spelling if he thought he'd discovered something important enough that he needed to notify the FBI?"

He wouldn't have been, of course. And Nick realized that he had no idea whether or not his father had been a good speller. One of the many things they had not gotten around to discussing, he thought with a touch of bitterness.

The DOA list that had been in his briefcase was still lying on the table. Cara opened it, revealing those daunting columns of names.

"God, even if that *were* it—"

"*Mc*'s and *Mac*'s. Look at those first," Nick suggested.

She obeyed, flipping pages and then running her finger down a column. "There are only two."

Maybe Miriam's suggestion was way off base. The fact that there were only a couple of *Mac*'s on the list, however, seemed to bode well for the search, at least.

"*Mac*'s aren't the only Scottish names," Miriam reminded them.

She was leaning against the counter by the coffeepot, the fragile skin under her eyes still showing the strain of the last few days combined with the late hours she'd spent on this last night.

"Wilson," Cara suggested. "Keith. And probably dozens of others I'm too tired to think of. This is pointless."

"Nicknames are usually given because of something that's fairly obvious, even to the casual observer. If they weren't, they wouldn't stick. That's especially true in the military. And since my dad remembered this one more than thirty years later, we have to assume it was commonly accepted."

Cara hadn't even waited for the completion of his argument. She had already flipped back to the page she'd been holding with her thumb.

"McGregor, Duncan. McMurray, Ray."

"Duncan McGregor," Miriam said. "Now that's a Scottish name if ever I've heard one. Even your father would have known it was Scottish."

It was at least somewhere to start, Nick acknowledged. He turned in his chair to take his cell phone from the pocket of his slacks and got a powerful reminder—as if he had needed one—of how much he wanted to find the people who'd arranged last night's hit-and-run.

"Address?" he asked as soon as he'd regained enough breath to allow him to speak.

Cara's eyes came up. "You said these were nearly thirty-five years old. You think he'd still be there."

"Probably not, but it's a place to start."

"Duncan McGregor, 812 Graham Hill Trace, Lockridge, Tennessee."

"Graham," Miriam said. "That's another one."

They both turned to look at her, apparently the same question in their eyes.

"Another Scottish name," she explained, her tone indicating that what she'd been talking about should be obvious to anyone. "Maybe that's a sign."

If it were, however, information in Lockridge, Tennessee, had no record of it. There was no Duncan McGregor listed in the phone book there.

"We need a map," Nick said, punching the off button on his cell.

"How will a map help?" Miriam asked.

"It will give us an area to work in. If Lockridge is a suburb of Nashville, for example, then we try metropolitan area information."

"This I *can* help with," Cara said, pushing her chair back from the table. "And I won't need to hack into anything protected to do it."

"The Internet," Miriam said smugly, well aware of her daughter's expertise. "They say you can find out anything about anybody these days."

"Especially if you have a birth date," Cara said, holding up the list Griff had secured from the Department of the Army. "Wherever this particular Duncan McGregor is, if he's still alive, we can find him."

Chapter Eight

Like Hiram Simonson and Nick's own father, the man they were hunting hadn't traveled far from his roots. Despite the mobility of the general population, most people of that generation were buried within a hundred miles of the place where they were born.

Duncan McGregor had been born in Lockridge, and as far as they had been able to determine, he hadn't yet been buried. If he *was* the Scottie on his father's list, they might just have gotten lucky, Nick thought as Cara drove the rental car they'd picked up at the Chattanooga airport along the winding mountain road.

He had halfheartedly tried to convince her not to come, but she had been more determined to see this through than he'd expected. She had also argued that she was the one who had located McGregor and that if this proved to be a wild-goose chase, he'd need her again to move on to the next Scots-sounding name on the list.

Besides, despite the fact that no other attempt had been made against his life during the less than twenty-four hours he'd spent at the Simonsons', Nick couldn't be sure that whoever had tried that botched hit-and-run was now targeting *only* him. In truth, he had known he'd feel better if Cara were where he could keep an eye on her.

She had convinced her mother to go to her aunt's, a visit that had already been scheduled to take place as soon as Cara returned to Washington. All they'd done was move it up a couple of days. They had watched Miriam guide the Mercedes out of the driveway this morning and then together they had headed for the airport.

Nick had tried several times to reach McGregor by phone, but all he'd gotten had been an answering machine. Not reassuring, especially when he remembered the message Crawford had left for his father. And he still didn't know whether the proposed meeting between the two of them had been at the FBI agent's instigation or his dad's.

When he'd closed out his father's account, the small, independent phone company that served the area had been able to give him a listing of the long-distance calls his father had made, including one to the Washington number of the FBI a few days before his death. They had explained, however, that they didn't keep a record of incoming calls on a landline—not unless law enforcement had requested in advance that they did.

"It can't be far now," Cara said, glancing over at him as she made the turn onto the narrow two-lane road where, according to the address she'd found on the Internet, Duncan McGregor lived.

By the time they'd gotten aboard the plane, it had been afternoon. The flight and the drive had taken long enough that dusk was falling over the Smoky Mountains, bringing with it the world famous mist.

"I think I'll try his number again. If he's been at work, he should be home by now."

There was still no answer, and Nick decided against leaving another message. They would be at the house in a few minutes, and the previous messages he'd left had been explicit enough to make sure McGregor understood the danger he was in. There seemed to be nothing else he could do at this point.

"Are you sure you don't want to contact the sheriff?" Cara asked.

He had debated that before they'd set out, but the evidence that had led Nick to the conclusion he'd reached hadn't been the kind law enforcement bought into. The three deaths he believed were murders had been officially listed as natural causes or accidents or suicide.

Besides, he had nothing concrete to go on in tying McGregor to the others. The cops would dismiss him as a crackpot and his concern that this particular man might be murdered as ludicrous. He knew that any token protection he could convince them to offer would be worse than useless.

"Let's see what we find when we get there."

The closer they came to their destination, the more apprehensive Nick felt. Whether that was the result of arriving too late to do anything for Cara's father or some premonition about McGregor, he couldn't be sure. All he knew was that his gut was telling him that something was about to go very wrong.

"It should be the next drive," Cara said, verifying the fluorescent numbers on the rural mailbox they had just passed from the notes she'd taken during her Internet search.

None of the houses along this stretch were visible

from the road. The narrow, unpaved turnoffs that led to them trailed away through thickets of pine.

Cara had slowed the car to a crawl, trying to find the next driveway. When she did, there was no mailbox to mark it, so she drove past and then had to back up.

"What do you think?" she asked, peering along the overgrown tract, which was almost hidden by foliage and the growing darkness.

Its unkempt condition made Nick unwillingly remember the neglected air of his father's place. Not really run-down, but certainly not maintained to the strict military standards his dad had demanded while Nick was growing up. The lawn not so closely mowed. The paint sun-faded and peeling in spots. McGregor's driveway had that same look.

"Turn in," he said shortly.

He had been trying to put his growing apprehension down to the same premission anticipation he always experienced. As they approached the small, wood-framed cabin, which fit into its surroundings so well it seemed almost a part of the rocks and the trees around it, he knew that this was something more. Everything—from the unanswered phone calls to the deserted appearance of the place—was setting off his well-tuned radar.

"No lights, but there's a pickup in the shed."

Cara's comment was made as she pulled the rental up to the end of the dirt road. Her hand closed around the key in the ignition, but she didn't turn it to shut off the engine.

"Nick?"

"Something's not right."

She turned to look at him, her eyes almost gray in

the failing light. "You feel that, too? I wasn't going to say anything, but…"

"Stay here," he ordered without responding to her confession.

She probably had him pegged as someone who didn't listen to those instinctive warnings. He had learned years ago, however, that anyone in his line of work who *didn't* listen to them usually ended up dead.

Dead. The word reverberated inside his head as he put his fingers around the door handle. He braced himself for the discomfort of getting out of the car, swinging his legs around first and then pulling his aching body up with his left hand on the top of the door and his right on the back of the seat. He had eased the door closed before he realized that Cara was already standing on the other side of the vehicle.

"What the hell are you doing?" he whispered, automatically responding to the absolute stillness of the clearing.

She was looking up at the cabin, which had been built into the side of the hill. A rough path led upward from the end of the drive where they were parked to the front door.

"I thought we settled this before we left this morning," she said, pulling her eyes away from the unlit house to look at him.

"There's no way to know what we may find up there."

If anything. It was always possible the place was as deserted as it appeared. Maybe Duncan McGregor had died of natural causes months ago.

Or maybe Nick had been wrong in thinking that their adversary was having to figure out the names on his father's list just as they were. Maybe Cara's father was the last of the intended victims rather than the second. Maybe the others were already all dead. Maybe his father had somehow gotten wind of their deaths, and that's why he'd called the FBI. Maybe everything he had thought he understood about this was wrong.

"Nick?"

Cara had probably said something to him while he'd been in the process of discarding all the things he thought he knew. That blanket rejection of his carefully constructed theory was way premature, he admitted. At least until they knew what was inside the cabin in front of them.

"Sorry. What did you say?"

"I said I don't want to stay out here. Not alone."

The half light of dusk was quickly giving way to night. Another fifteen minutes and they wouldn't be able to distinguish anything in their surroundings but shapes.

"Back the car down the drive and then pull it in so the headlights shine up on the house and the path," Nick ordered.

Trying to ignore the soreness in his side, he bent and retrieved his semiautomatic. He had checked it through in his bag, but as soon as they'd picked up the rental car, he'd taken it out and put it inside the glove box.

Straightening with a grimace, he stepped away from the car. Cara had already gotten back inside and started the engine. As she backed up, positioning the car as he'd instructed her, the headlights provided an eerie, uneven illumination, less kind to the small cabin than twilight had been.

If McGregor was inside, he hadn't responded either to the sound of a vehicle driving into his front yard or to the light now shining through his front windows. As isolated as his home was, that lack of response didn't make a lot of sense. Again, anxiety tightened Nick's stomach.

"Nick?"

Cara was once more standing outside the car, looking at him over the roof. Whatever he found in that cabin, she would have to know eventually.

And she was right. Leaving her out here alone in the darkness wasn't an acceptable alternative.

"Come on," he said, heading toward the path.

He was holding his arm against his side by the time they reached the narrow porch. He could hear Cara's breathing behind him as he climbed, but he'd been forced to concentrate on putting one foot in front of the other, trying to focus on anything other than the pain.

He stepped onto the porch's wooden flooring, his heels echoing in the unnatural silence. He adjusted the hold of his fingers around the weapon, an attempt to relieve some of the tension that had caused him to grip it too hard. Then he lifted his left hand to knock on the door.

He waited, aware that Cara was standing as close to him as she could without physically touching him. Just as he had down below, she was reacting to the atmosphere of the place.

By now, he had resigned himself to the worst. He just wanted to get this over as quickly as possible. He would report whatever they found to the local authorities, and then try to beat whoever was behind this string of murders to the next victim.

As the stillness stretched uncomfortably, Nick knocked again, calling out this time. "Mr. McGregor? Are you here?"

The silence in the clearing was profound, despite the fall of darkness. There were no sounds from the night creatures, who would normally be filling the air with their distinctive noises.

"Mr. McGregor?"

Cara stepped over to the window that flanked the right side of the front door. Cupping her hand, she put the outside of it against the glass and then leaned her forehead against her thumb.

"Too dark to see anything," she said after a moment. "The place seems deserted. Maybe we should go back and check with someone in the nearest town. Maybe he's moved. Or…"

Or maybe he's dead. It was the same thought Nick had had earlier.

Maybe the homestead seemed abandoned because it had been. And maybe this was exactly the wild-goose chase Cara had warned him about.

"Let's check around back," Nick suggested.

That wasn't something he wanted to do. He wanted to get back into the car and get the hell out of here. They'd already come this far, however, and given the very limited information they'd had to work with, McGregor had seemed their best bet. If this didn't work out—

He banished the thought as defeatist and stepped off the porch to walk around the side of the cabin. There was less light from the headlights there, and he knew there would be even less at the back. *Wild-goose chase* echoed in his brain.

He glanced back to find Cara following him. She was using the outside wall of the cabin as a guide, her right hand maintaining contact with the rough planks as she walked. It was probably safer, given the darkness, but he was unwilling to either put the semiauto-matic away or to shift it to his left hand.

He stopped when he reached the rear corner of the house. Staying close to the wall, he eased forward far enough to look along the back.

He'd been right about the lack of light here. Cut off from even the moonlight by the rise of the hill behind the cabin, it was impossible to see more than a few feet in front of him.

Cara bumped into him in the darkness. He could hear the small intake of breath that signaled her sur-prise.

"Shh…" he cautioned, putting his left arm back to keep her behind him.

She was standing close enough that he could feel the warmth of her breath against his neck. Close enough that he was aware of the fragrance of her per-fume—something faintly floral—just as he'd been when she'd put his arm over her shoulder last night.

"What is it?"

The words were whispered against his ear, as she laid her hand on the top of his shoulder. He could feel her breasts pressed against his back. Despite the sense of danger that had been plaguing him since they'd turned into the drive, he reacted physically to her near-ness.

He eased a breath, trying to get his mind back on task. Wordlessly, he shook his head, knowing that she was close enough to feel the movement even if she couldn't see it.

His eyes having adjusted to the lack of light, he scanned the area behind the house. Nothing moved among the shadows. Nothing seemed out of place.

He stepped forward, Cara's hand still on his shoulder. He edged along the back wall, looking for another entrance to the place. He took a moment to try to see into one of the windows they passed, as Cara had, but the glass was cold and black.

When he located the back door, he stopped, putting his ear against its solid wood. Even if someone were inside, he probably wouldn't be able to hear movement through its thickness.

"Mr. McGregor?" he called again.

Once more they waited, holding their breaths through the resulting stillness. And again there was no answer.

Close to Nick's feet was a dark shape that looked as if it might be a bucket. He stooped, lifting it with his left hand, surprised by its weight.

He discovered that instead of one of the modern galvanized pails, this was made of wooden staves attached to a round bottom and bound together with a couple of metal strips. It made an awkward knocker, but he used it now against the heavy door. The clangs it made echoed throughout the clearing.

"Mr. McGregor? Are you there?"

"Try the door," Cara whispered.

It was the same conclusion he'd come to. If the man they'd come to find *was* inside, he was obviously dead or incapacitated. No one could sleep through that ungodly hammering.

Of course, he was also aware that this was an area where people shot first and asked questions later. There were probably more shotguns and rifles in these mountains than there were dishwashers or washing machines. Still…

"Stay here," he ordered.

He set the bucket down and moved to the other

side of the door, putting the fingers of his left hand around the doorknob. Before he turned it, he looked across at Cara, still on the opposite side, watching him. All he could see in the darkness was the pale oval of her face.

He tightened his grip on the knob and turned it, no longer surprised to feel it move under his hand. As the door swung open a few inches, everything seemed to happen at once.

The unmistakable smell of propane gas poured through the narrow opening he'd created and out into the cooler night air. Almost before his brain had time to identify the distinctive and terrifying scent, there was a subtle pop and then a flare from somewhere in the front of the cabin.

By that time Nick had already begun to move. He leaped across the porch, somehow managing to get his left arm around Cara to pull her with him. He had taken no more than three or four running steps when the house exploded behind them.

The concussive wave knocked them both off their feet, throwing them forward toward the foot of the hill. Adrenaline roaring through his bloodstream, Nick never even thought about his previous injuries. As soon as he hit the ground, he began crawling across the hard-packed dirt until his searching hands encountered the warmth and softness of the woman he'd brought with him.

He scrambled over her, using his body as a shield, as flaming debris fell over and around them. Deafened by the first explosion, he felt rather than heard the shock wave of the second. He lowered his head over Cara's, who lay unmoving beneath him, and prayed to feel the rise and fall of her breathing.

Chapter Nine

The long, slow inhalation was an answer to his prayer. After a moment Cara coughed, moving slightly under his weight.

Alive. And breathing.

Something hot landed on his back. He reached over his shoulder to knock the still-smoldering object off. As he did, Cara raised her head, trying to turn to the side to look up at him. He lifted his right hand, surprised to find he was still holding the Glock, and pushed her back down.

Then, to offer as much protection as he could, he put his forehead over her temple and wrapped his arm around the top of her head. Still deafened by the explosion, he couldn't hear the fire behind him, but he could feel it. Although things were still falling out of the sky, the heat was becoming unbearable. For a second or two, he couldn't decide which was the greater risk: to keep Cara safe from the flaming debris by holding her under him or to try to make a run for the car.

She moved again, struggling to get her head up. He shifted so that she could lift her upper body off the ground, but he continued to shield her from the fall-out of the burning cabin.

She turned, looking at him again over her shoulder. In the crimsoned light from the inferno behind him, her eyes were wide and dark in her paper-white face. Her mouth was open as she tried to get oxygen from the smoke-filled air.

"You hurt?"

He hadn't been able to hear his own question, but Cara shook her head. He wasn't sure if that was an answer to what he'd asked or a signal that she hadn't been able to hear it. In any case, with the growing intensity of the heat, he knew they had no choice but to get out of here.

Operating off the adrenaline rush he'd experienced when he'd seen the flash that set off the explosion, he didn't know whether or not he'd been injured in the blast. As he got to his feet, however, everything seemed to be fully functional. All he could be sure of was the loss of hearing.

He reached down and put his hand around Cara's arm to help her stand. He didn't attempt any other questions. Once she was up, he used his hands to signal his intent to head back to the car.

As they began to retrace their steps around the side of the cabin, she stumbled over the rough ground. When he tried to stop to see if she were hurt, she pulled against his hold, moving determinedly away from the conflagration behind them. Once he had to brush a burning piece of debris from her hair.

As they rounded the corner, Nick was almost surprised to find the rental car still sitting on the incline, headlights shining up the slope. He couldn't tell if it had been damaged, but as long as it would start, it didn't matter. Not at this point.

"What about McGregor?"

He wasn't sure how much of Cara's question he had lip-read and how much he'd actually heard, although he thought he could now hear the faint roar of the fire behind them. He shook his head, urging her along with him toward the car.

"Nick."

She resisted his direction, stopping and looking back at the burning cabin instead. That was all it took to force her to the same conclusion Nick had already reached. Even if McGregor had been inside, there was nothing they could do for him now.

And that had obviously been the intent of whoever had filled his cabin with gas and then rigged some mechanism that would set it off when the door was opened.

THE FIRST OF THE locals arrived before Nick could get the car turned around and headed back down the drive. He cursed his luck that someone had made it to the cabin this quickly.

Being found at the scene of the explosion narrowed their options for accomplishing their mission, which had been difficult enough already. Given little choice, other than setting off a statewide manhunt, Nick stopped beside the arriving pickup and rolled down his window. The sunburned face of the teenage driver was both concerned and curious.

"Gas leak," Nick said in response to a question he couldn't quite hear.

"…volunteer fire department."

Nick wasn't sure about the first part of whatever the kid had said, but he definitely got the impression the boy had not come to sightsee, but rather to fight the fire. Apparently not only did the kid live close, he was also eager. A new volunteer maybe. Or maybe they didn't get this kind of opportunity very often around here.

"Anybody inside?" The kid's question was easier to lip-read because Nick had been expecting it.

"I don't know. We were looking for Duncan McGregor. He still live here?"

The boy turned to look at the flames shooting sky-ward from the shell of the cabin so that Nick missed most of his answer. When the kid turned to face him again, Nick cupped his hand behind his ear.

"Can't hear too well. Explosion."

The volunteer nodded his understanding. "That's Duncan's place all right," he yelled.

"You think he was here?"

"His pickup's in the shed," the kid said. "Old Dunc don't go *nowhere* without his truck."

Cara put her hand on Nick's arm, leaning across him to pose her own question to the boy. "Isn't there something we can do?"

The look in the kid's eyes was answer enough, but he shrugged, as well. "Maybe when the trucks get here…"

As if in answer to that, an ancient tanker turned into the drive. Only when it headed toward them did Nick hear its siren, although it would obviously have been blaring throughout its journey.

The teen quickly pulled his pickup off the shoulder of the drive to let the tanker by. The firefighters on board looked at the rental car with the same open cu-riosity the kid had displayed. Before the fire truck reached the inferno that had been Duncan McGre-gor's home, a sheriff's cruiser made the turn off the highway, followed by another, equally outdated tanker.

The cruiser pulled up behind the boy's pickup, allowing the second fire truck to speed by, its siren blaring. The kid got out and walked back to the sheriff's car. As they talked through the open window, the volunteer firefighter gestured toward Nick.

After a moment he came back to their car. "Buck wants to talk to you. He said to tell you to pull up to the turnaround."

Already resigned to answering questions, Nick turned the car and drove back toward the cabin, parking at a safe distance from the blaze. Although the structure was totally engulfed by flames, that didn't prevent the volunteers from going through the motions.

However lacking their equipment, there was no denying their training or dedication. The hoses were spraying water from the big tanks in a matter of minutes.

Nick got out of the car, pretending to watch them, all the while knowing that a confrontation with the local authorities was inevitable. After all, he had been discovered on the scene of a fire that was eventually going to be ruled arson.

He was about to face a lot of questions, some of which he had no answers for. He could only hope that whoever was in charge would believe what had brought him here.

As the firefighters battled the fire, the deputy who had followed the trucks to the scene got out of his cruiser and started across the hard-packed dirt of the clearing in front of the house.

"What are you going to tell him?"

Cara was still sitting in the car with the window rolled down, despite the smoke. The volunteers had now begun spraying the trees around the clearing since the house was obviously too far gone for their efforts to make any difference.

"The truth," Nick said.

It was something Griff had taught them when dealing with interrogation. Tell as much of the truth as you can without putting the team in danger or breaching national security.

Neither of those came into play in this case. And the only chance Nick had to keep from being charged with arson and murder was to make the case that someone else had already carried out both before he and Cara arrived.

"YOU GOT ANY proof of all this?"

The deputy had listened without comment throughout Nick's recital. It was difficult to tell from the lean, hard-bitten face whether or not he had believed it.

"I don't have their death certificates, if that's what you mean. I would imagine, given the nature of the deaths, that you could get the information from law enforcement in the respective areas."

"Except that ain't gonna tell me anything except that those folks died. And according to you, everybody else is satisfied there wasn't any foul play involved."

"Don't forget Special Agent Crawford's death," Cara said.

"Begging your pardon, ma'am, but I just don't find heart attacks all that suspicious."

"How about arson?"

With Nick's question, the deputy looked back at the burned-out shell of the cabin. "*If* that's the finding. 'A course, who done that would still be open to question, wouldn't it?"

"If you want references, I can provide them," Nick said.

"You got *those* on you?" There was a thread of amusement in the question.

"They're as near as a telephone and a fax machine."

"Well, those would be down at the sheriff's office."

Nick had known since the volunteers' arrival on the scene had prevented them from getting away without being seen that a visit to the local law enforcement department was probably inevitable. That didn't keep it from being frustrating.

"We got here too late to save Duncan McGregor. There are three other names on the list my father left. The longer we're delayed answering questions, the more likely it is that we'll be too late for them, too."

"If what you say is true, seems like you folks might welcome some help. Why don't you turn the information you got over to the authorities and let them handle it?"

"You're willing to do that?"

With Cara's question the deputy turned back to her, his eyes considering. "I'm willing to let you lay out your case."

"We just did," Nick said.

"I mean with evidence. Whatever documentation you got that these deaths were what *you* say they are, rather than what the attending coroners or medical examiners judged 'em to be. Once I've seen the evidence, and you've established a connection between the three of them—"

"If we had that kind of proof, we would have gone to the authorities in the first place." Nick no longer bothered to hide his frustration.

"Which would have meant you wouldn't be a suspect to arson right now."

"Look—"

"'A course, if what you're saying about somebody wanting to kill Dunc is true, and we find out he *is* in that house…" The deputy inclined his head toward the smoldering pile that had been McGregor's home. "I guess that would make you a suspect to a murder, as well. All I know right now is that you two aren't going anywhere until the state fire marshal can get up here and make a finding."

"Are you *arresting* us?" The tone of her question again brought the deputy's gaze back to Cara.

"No, ma'am. I'm just saying that you two aren't going to be leaving Bassett County until we know a whole lot more about what happened here than we do right now. There's a motel on the highway. The department budget will stretch to cover a deputy on duty there to make sure you don't get antsy to get back to this 'mission' you all are on. Leastways not until the sheriff's satisfied you didn't have nothing to do with what happened in his jurisdiction."

"Do you really have references?"

Cara knew Nick had placed a couple of phone calls from the sheriff's office, but she hadn't been let in on the results. Other than the fact that they were still here.

He looked up from the process of carefully removing the pickles from one of the half-dozen hamburgers a deputy had just delivered to their motel room. His eyes were rimmed with red, and there were circles under them so dark that they looked like bruises. A long, angry burn marred one bewhiskered cheek. Another ran across the knuckle of the hand with which he held the thin burger.

"A couple."

"Are they good enough to get us out of here?"

"Probably. Eventually."

She waited, watching as he put the top of the bun back over the gray meat and took a bite. He didn't offer to elaborate on his connections who he believed might extricate them from this situation.

"You think McGregor was in that house?"

He looked up again, his eyes contemplating her face. After a moment, he laid the burger down on the paper it had been wrapped in.

"Yes."

"Then why didn't he answer the door?"

The image of the man they'd come to rescue burning to death while they stood helplessly outside was one she didn't want in her head. It was there, however, now reinforced by Nick's affirmation.

"Because he was already dead."

"But…" She paused, thinking about the implications of that. "Then why trigger that explosion?"

The dark eyes remained on her face, but Nick didn't answer. Obviously she was supposed to figure this out on her own. And the only thing that made sense…

"You think that was meant for us," she said softly, arriving at the conclusion Nick had reached long ago. That's why he had insisted on their sharing a room, despite the look that request had evoked from the deputy who'd brought them into town. "You think they're still here?"

"I think they know that we're doing the same thing they're doing. Trying to track down the people on my father's list. They knew we'd find McGregor. Your mother was right. It was the obvious connection. And when we finally made it, the gas and the explosion would be waiting for us."

"For how long?"

"I don't know. I'm no expert, but I would think without a spark to set it off, the house could have been set up like that for a while. Or they could have done it this afternoon."

"Which would mean they aren't that far ahead of us," she said, feeling a surge of satisfaction despite the tragedy that had unfolded that afternoon.

Nick had said he had been twenty-four hours too late to save her dad. If they had managed to cut the gap to only a few hours—

"Or that they know exactly where we are and what we're doing," he said, picking the hamburger up again. This time he brought it to his mouth and took a bite.

She wondered if it tasted as much like cardboard as hers. She had forced herself to eat half of it and a few fries simply because once again she couldn't remember the last time she'd eaten and because she knew that she would eventually be sick if she didn't eat something.

"I don't understand," she said as she watched him chew. "I thought you'd believed all along that they knew we were trying to figure out the list."

"I mean *exactly* what we're doing. When we bought our airline tickets and to where. When we rented the car."

"How could they know that?"

"I don't *know* that they do. It just feels like a possibility."

There were certainly ways of doing that, as anyone in her field could attest. And it wouldn't have to be an official kind of surveillance. There were plenty of people sophisticated enough to track that kind of information through the computers. The records of all of the things Nick had mentioned would be contained in some system. And none of it could be considered particularly secure information.

"What do we do next?"

She couldn't remember a time in her life when she had felt so little in control of what was happening to her—from the moment her mother had called with the news about her father's death to Nick's question at the wake to the hit-and-run attempt on their lives. And, of course, with tonight's fire and explosions.

Those kinds of things didn't happen to her. They happened to other people. Her life was controlled. And incredibly ordinary. At least it had been until Nick Morelli had shown up.

"We do the only thing we *can* do right now. We eat and then we try to get some sleep."

He took another bite of the hamburger and chewed it almost stoically. This obviously wasn't the first time he'd been in a situation like this. And the advice he'd just given her, no matter how ridiculous it seemed in the face of what they'd been through, was probably smart.

He might even be able to carry it out. He'd eat what he had been given, and then he'd crawl into one of the two double beds and close his eyes and go to sleep.

Maybe he wouldn't see the flames or hear the explosion. Maybe he could shut it all out of his consciousness. She knew that she wouldn't be able to.

All night long she would smell the acrid scent of smoke and feel the intensity of the heat. And she would think about the man who had been inside that burning cabin, as well as the one who had been inside the car they had pulled up from the bottom of that ravine.

Chapter Ten

Nick had let her have the bathroom first, a gesture she appreciated. After she'd washed the smell of smoke out of her hair and scrubbed it off her skin, she stood under the stream of hot water for a long time, letting it pound over her shoulders and the top of her spine.

Maybe she was trying to wash away her exhaustion or the horror of what had occurred. Or maybe she was postponing the moment when she would have to walk back into the motel room she was sharing with a man who was virtually a stranger.

Despite the time they had spent together, he was still a stranger, she acknowledged as she dried her hair on one of the motel's thick white towels. Nick Morelli was as much an enigma to her now as when he had walked across the living room of her mother's house and forced her out onto the sunporch. Considering that they were on the verge of being arrested for murder, maybe it was time she asked him the questions that had been building in her mind since he had gotten her involved in this.

Just not tonight, she decided when she walked out of the bathroom and found him lying on the double bed closest to the door. He hadn't bothered to pull down the spread or to take off his charred shirt. It looked as if he had simply collapsed.

His eyes were closed, his arms crossed almost protectively over his abdomen. For the first time in hours she remembered the bruised ribs. In spite of that very painful injury, he had probably saved her life tonight. *Again.*

"All yours," she said.

She had thought about putting on the change of clothing she'd brought in her overnight bag rather than her nightshirt. In the end she had decided that would be too much a confession of the discomfort she felt over sharing the room.

She knew Nick had suggested this as a precaution, despite the presence of the deputy outside. She didn't want him to think that she was making a big deal about a situation that was in no way intended to be intimate.

Except by its very nature...

In response to her announcement about the availability of the bathroom, Nick began to sit up, doing it in careful stages so that she knew she'd been right. He was in pain. Judging by the way he was moving, a lot of it.

When he was almost upright on the side of the bed, he glanced over to where she was still hovering near the bathroom door. Ridiculously, she felt like she had the first time she'd worn a bikini. Far too exposed.

"Feel better?" he asked.

"Cleaner, at least. I hope I left you enough hot water."

The motel had been much nicer than she'd expected from the very rural setting. It was fairly new, and both the bathroom and the carpet seemed clean. Maybe the hot water supply would be in keeping with the rest.

"It'll be fine." He stood, wincing as he slowly straightened his body.

"Ribs?"

"Among various and sundry other things."

"'Various and sundry'?" she repeated, fighting a smile. It didn't seem like something he would say.

"My mother used to say that. I have no idea what it means."

"Exactly how you used it, I think."

He nodded. He still hadn't moved away from the bed. And she hadn't stepped away from the doorway to the bathroom.

Despite the fact that he looked like he'd been to hell and back, for some reason she was suddenly very conscious again of his absolute maleness. Even more so than she had been last night, watching as her mother had cut off his shirt to reveal that flat, brown belly with its tantalizing arrow of dark hair.

His eyes hadn't left hers but, as a woman, she knew that he was aware of what she had on. Of how *little* she had on, she amended, her mouth going dry as it had last night.

The nightshirt had been a mistake. She had known that, and yet she had put it on anyway, refusing to admit to the sexual tension that had been between them almost from the instant his hand had closed around her arm.

Nick Morelli was something outside her experience. Just like the explosion tonight. Just like answering questions in a police station.

It was all new and dangerous and frightening. Maybe what those dark eyes were doing to her heart rate was the most frightening of all.

"Stop worrying," he said, obviously sensing her anxiety.

"I'm not used to being a suspect. Or a target."

"*Those* you can worry about. Be my guest. That isn't what I was talking about."

She swallowed, realizing that he knew exactly what she'd been thinking. She wasn't normally that transparent. Not with men. Of course, he wasn't exactly the kind of man she was used to dealing with, either.

"Then…what *are* you talking about?"

That's it. Pretend you don't know. Ask to be embarrassed. Make a bigger fool of yourself than you already have.

"I'm not going to try to make love to you."

Straightforward enough that she couldn't possibly pretend not to understand. Despite his bluntness, despite how right he was in his assessment, for some stupid reason she couldn't leave it alone. She couldn't just nod and walk across the room and crawl into her own bed like the chastened child she felt like right now.

"I never thought you were."

The mobile corner of his mouth moved slightly. Again, that lift was too subtle to be classified as a smile, but the blush that had started along her throat climbed higher as she watched it.

She had never actually noticed his lips before, she realized. In contrast to the lean cheeks and narrow, almost aquiline nose, they weren't thin or hard. Especially the bottom one. It was full. Sensuous. Made for kissing.

"Just as long as we're clear," he said.

Crystal.

She couldn't remember what movie that exchange had come from, but it seemed appropriate. She did manage to refrain from saying it aloud.

"Of course," she said instead.

She started across the room, heading for the other bed. As she walked, she was too aware of everything that was happening. Sensitive to every nuance. The heat in her cheeks. The feel of the carpet under her bare feet. The cold air from the AC unit against her exposed legs. The fact that he was moving toward her.

She had headed toward the far side of the other bed, which meant that she should be well out of his way before he reached the doorway. Deliberately, she didn't look at him. Part embarrassment. Part anger, maybe. Definitely confusion.

Still, she wasn't surprised when his hand closed around her upper arm, stopping her in midstride. She looked down at it rather than at his face, trying to make the point that he had no right to restrain her.

Something about those long brown fingers, so damnably masculine against the paleness of her skin, prevented her from expressing her anger. They were slightly callused. A little rough. Incredibly strong.

And along the back of them was the angry red mark she'd noticed before. Acquired while shielding her from the falling debris? Or in brushing that flaming splinter of wood out of her hair?

Her throat closed over the angry words she had been about to say. She couldn't have pushed them past its sudden constriction, even if she had wanted to.

She didn't. Not anymore.

She looked up, straight into his eyes. She didn't notice the tiredness in them as she had before. All she saw was their intensity. *And his hunger.*

Her heart hesitated, and then began beating far too rapidly. Heat spread like hot honey through her lower body. Her lips parted slightly and then closed. Her eyes never broke contact with his.

"When I make love to you, it won't be in some cheap motel. And I won't be moving like some stove-up rodeo hotshot."

The image evoked by those last words was both erotic and powerful. She didn't even know if that's what he had intended or if his word choice was simply a matter of some past experience.

She could see him doing that. Riding those fiercely bucking horses. Or the bulls. She could see him doing almost anything that was dangerous and exciting.

That was his life. What he had just promised would happen between them—and she had no doubt that had been a promise—meant that she would have become a part of it. Whether she wanted to or not.

And if he made love to her, then he would leave his mark on her soul, as surely as they burned brands into the flesh of the animals in the rodeo. Nick Morelli wasn't the kind of man a woman would ever be able to forget.

She realized she was still staring up at him, her heart beating so hard that he must be able to see its pulse in her throat. She tightened her lips, pressing them together so that nothing of what she had been thinking could slip out.

And then, using the last ounce of willpower she possessed, she broke the eye contact between them, again looking down at his fingers, which were still wrapped around her arm. She said nothing, not trusting herself to speak.

After a moment he freed her, stepping back and then continuing on his way to the bathroom as if nothing had happened. As soon as she heard the door slam behind him, she closed her eyes, allowing her body to sag a little from the rigidity she had imposed upon it.

Then she opened them again to look down at her arm. The red marks his fingers had made were already fading, but it was as if she could still feel them there. Warm and hard. Controlling.

Nick wasn't a man who asked. He was a man who took. Command. Control. Whatever he wanted.

And he had just made it very clear that he wanted her.

Crystal.

AFTER A COUPLE of hours, Cara decided that Nick was an exceptionally sound sleeper. She had expected at least the occasional snore or restive changing of position. She had certainly done enough of the latter.

As far as she could tell, however, he hadn't moved since he'd crawled into bed. In the stillness, she listened to his breathing, as slow and regular as a heartbeat.

Apparently none of the images that ran through her brain when she closed her eyes troubled Nick. Maybe experience with death and dying did that to you. Maybe you no longer worried about things you couldn't change.

She turned over again, trying to make as little noise as possible. She lay on her right side, using her fist to punch her pillow into a more comfortable position underneath her cheek.

Then, eyes wide, she watched the numbers tick over on the digital display of the motel's clock radio. And she listened to Nick breathe.

After a long time, she took a deep breath and then released it with a small whooshing sound. The sigh certainly wasn't loud enough to wake anyone, not even someone sleeping two feet away. Not if they were sleeping as soundly as Nick seemed to be.

"What's wrong?"

The deep voice from the darkness touched a chord within her chest. Somehow, disembodied, it seemed calming rather than anxiety producing.

"I can't sleep," she said unnecessarily. "Too much has happened, I guess."

There was a small silence. She waited through it, wondering if his response would be to blow off her jitters.

"The first time is always the worst."

The first time you watch someone die? That certainly made sense in the context of what had happened tonight.

"Do you think they'll lay a trap for us the next time?"

"If we don't get there first."

"But how can we? Unless you've had some revelation in the last few hours."

"The only revelation I've had lately is that neither of us is getting any sleep. Actually, that wasn't a revelation. I've known it for quite a while."

"You didn't move." The words sounded like an accusation.

"Yeah, well, we all make choices."

It took her a minute. He hadn't moved because he chose not to. Because it was painful?

She'd been tossing and turning, envying him his ability to sleep so soundly. He'd been lying perfectly still because he was too bruised and battered to do anything else.

"Is that why you can't sleep?"

Another silence, this one stretching a long time.

"Nick?"

It seemed she had said his name a dozen times today with that same questioning inflection. Asking what they should do next. Pleading for reassurance.

"Not entirely, but…it's a good enough reason for government work."

"Did your mom say that, too?"

"My dad." She could hear the amusement in his voice. "He didn't have much respect for bureaucrats."

"Neither did mine. Maybe the army did that to them."

He didn't answer, letting the room grow still except for the low hum of the air conditioner. Maybe he didn't want to talk anymore. After all, this seemed like such a feminine kind of thing. Lying in bed talking. Like a slumber party.

At least that image was safe. Unlike the one he had introduced a couple of hours ago. Sweating cowboys riding bucking horses.

With the memory, she knew that she didn't want to let him stop talking. If neither of them was going to sleep anyway…

"You were in the army."

"Uh-huh."

Not very encouraging, but then she had little to lose. If she stopped asking questions, then she would be alone again in the nightmare-tinged blackness. Alone, even with him in the bed right next to hers.

"Is that who's going to give you a reference?"

He laughed, the sound harsh and then abruptly cut off as he caught his breath. Apparently laughter hurt as much as any other kind of movement.

"Sorry. I didn't mean to make you laugh."

No answer. She resisted trying to prompt him by saying his name again. A dozen times in one day was surely enough.

"Does that mean they *wouldn't* give you a reference?"

Dishonorable discharge? He had said he didn't last long enough to make it a career as his father had. Maybe the army had kicked him out. Nick didn't seem to be the kind who would suffer fools gladly, and she imagined the military had its share of those.

"That means it probably wouldn't have any effect if they did."

"On the sheriff?"

"I imagine most people in this county spent some time in the service. Probably even the ones in his jail."

Military service was a tradition in the South, more so than in any other part of the country. And an even longer tradition in these mountains.

"Then who?"

"Some people I know."

"People you worked with."

"At one time."

Law enforcement? If he had been a cop, that would explain a lot of things. The way he'd approached McGregor's place tonight. The gun. The air of competence, no matter the situation.

"And now?"

"Now I work in private enterprise."

Which might mean anything. It was clear that he was unwilling to share any information he didn't absolutely have to. Either with the sheriff or with her. Of course, he hadn't had any choice in the former. And if he could tell them...

"What kind of enterprise?"

A beat of silence.

"Private investigation."

It sounded like something out of one of those paperbacks her father used to read. Again, it was an occupation that seemed to have no connection to her own life, but at least it explained all the things she had wondered about.

"Have you done that long?"

"A little over five years."

"From the time you got out of the army?"

"After a couple of side trips."

"Can you tell me about any of those?"

"No."

There had been nothing harsh about the tone of the refusal, but it had clearly been unequivocal. Apparently they had reached the end of any confidences Nick was willing to make. It was probably more than she should have expected.

"If you don't get some sleep, you won't be able to function tomorrow."

An attempt to soften that abrupt refusal? Also more than she had expected.

"So what do we do tomorrow?"

"The same thing we've been doing. We try to figure out the next person on the list. And we try to do that before they do."

They. Whoever had murdered her father and his. Whoever had filled Duncan McGregor's cabin with gas and rigged it to blow when they opened the door. Whoever had arranged Don Crawford's heart attack.

The nameless, faceless they, who were always, it seemed, one step ahead of them.

Chapter Eleven

"Seems like you've got friends in high places."

Sheriff Polk's comment didn't sound like a compliment. However it was meant, Cara felt a surge of relief when she heard it. Apparently Nick's references had come through for him.

"A few."

After another long, hot shower this morning, Nick seemed to be moving better. That had not been the case when he had risen from his bed in slow stages at dawn. Pretending to be asleep, she had watched through her lashes as he'd limped into the bathroom.

He had emerged, more than half an hour later, not only shaved and dressed in fresh clothes, but obviously much less stiff. He'd made coffee in the motel's coffeemaker, which had given her an excuse to "come awake."

The knock on the door had occurred perhaps fifteen minutes later. The deputy, who waited patiently for her to dress before taking them down to the sheriff's office, had treated them with a deference that had been missing last night. That had been her first clue that however reticent Nick was to talk about his past, he had been right about the influence of the people he'd called to vouch for him.

"CIA, huh?" the sheriff went on. "Musta been interesting work."

"At times."

Obviously Nick wasn't going to be any more forthcoming with the man than he had been with her. At least now she knew what he'd been doing during those years between the army and the private enterprise he'd mentioned.

Again, it fit. All the things people normally thought of when the Agency was mentioned seemed right down Nick's alley. Clandestine missions. Black ops. Down and dirty intelligence gathering. Things that made him imminently suited for the task he'd undertaken. If anyone could track down his father's killer, Nick could.

"Then we're free to go?" Nick asked, interrupting that train of thought.

Lips pursed, Sheriff Polk pretended to think about the question. It was obvious he was reluctant to release them before the investigation was finished, but it was equally clear that he had been genuinely impressed by whoever had responded to Nick's phone call.

"I'd appreciate it if you'd hang around until tomorrow," he said finally. "The fire marshal will be here this afternoon. He may have some questions the two of you could answer. After all, you aren't denying that you sparked that explosion. Got any ideas how it was rigged?"

"Some kind of counterweight, maybe," Nick suggested. "The door opens, relieving pressure on something that drops, pulling a lever or turning a switch. All you'd need would be a wire connected to a flashlight battery or a broken lightbulb."

Polk nodded as if that made sense. "Trying to destroy whatever evidence they might've left."

"The fire did that, all right, but... I think they wanted *us* to open that door. They know we're trying to get to the other people on that list before they do. This way they kill two birds with one stone."

"You try the front door of McGregor's cabin?"

"No, but I'd be willing to bet it was also unlocked and rigged in the same way. My impression—and that's all it is, you understand—was that the spark came from the front of the house."

"They thought you'd open that door."

"And if we didn't, whoever eventually came looking for McGregor would. *Somebody* was going to open one of them, conveniently leaving very little evidence for you or anyone else to find."

"I meant what I said," Polk said again, obviously as impressed by Nick's explanation as his references. "I'd really appreciate it if you'd talk to the folks from Nashville when they get here."

Nick's eyes met hers, but Cara wasn't sure what he was looking for. He hadn't asked her permission for any of the decisions he'd made thus far, so she couldn't imagine why he would be seeking it now.

"We can probably arrange that," he said without waiting for her answer. "In the meantime, is there anyone in the area McGregor was close to? Anyone he might have talked to if something was bothering him?"

"Dunc? Hell, I doubt he's talked to half a dozen people in this county during the last twenty years. McGregor was a real loner. His family always kept to themselves, but he had solitude down to a science. Folks say 'Nam changed him. I don't know. I don't remember him from before. I just know he was one ornery son of a bitch. Beg your pardon, ma'am. Whoever took out old Dunc would have had their hands full. That much you can count on."

THE SHERIFF HAD DRIVEN them up to McGregor's cabin later in the afternoon to meet with the fire marshal. A couple of technicians were shifting through the ashes when they arrived. Wisps of smoke still drifted upward from parts of the ruins.

The inspector's questions had been both pointed and extensive. He had seemed particularly interested in the flash Nick had seen from the front of the cabin, nodding as he described it.

He had also listened politely as, at Sheriff Polk's insistence, Nick had repeated the ways in which he theorized the explosion could have been set off. The entire time he'd talked, Nick had felt as if he were being evaluated.

Apparently whatever the fire marshal's criteria for credibility were, he passed, which resulted in a guided tour of the fire. A tour that had included the location where the remains of McGregor's body had been found.

Although that didn't really help him in knowing how to proceed from here, Nick had been interested in the information. He'd become concerned, however, about the obvious impact of the fire marshal's sometimes grisly narrative on Cara.

She hadn't said a word on the trip back to the motel. Even the sheriff had commented on her quietness after she'd gotten out of the car.

"It's been a stressful few days," Nick said, leaning down to speak through the open window on the driver's side.

Even as he offered the explanation, he realized

what an understatement it was. Cara had been faced with her father's unexpected death, quickly followed by Nick's contention that it hadn't been an accident, as she'd thought, but a murder. Almost immediately after that had been the first attack against them, the hit-and-run at the barbecue place and then last night's explosion. It was no wonder she was in emotional overload.

"You take care of her, you hear," Polk ordered gruffly, his gaze following as she walked toward the motel.

Nick straightened, leaving his hand on the bottom of the window frame a second while he considered the command. The fact that he felt responsible for Cara must be apparent even to the casual observer like Polk. Maybe the rest of what he was beginning to feel for her was too obvious, as well.

"I'll do my best," he said. "I take it we're free to leave?"

"I got your card. Reckon I can catch up with you if I need to."

"Thanks."

"Good luck," Polk said, shifting the cruiser into Reverse. "Sounds like you all are gonna need it."

The sheriff was probably right, Nick thought as he crossed the strip of parking lot. Since he had the only key, Cara was waiting for him beside the decorative wrought-iron column that gave access to the covered walkway leading to their room.

He put his hand against the small of her back, urging her through the opening ahead of him. As they neared the first of the rooms on the ground floor, there was a loud bang from the street behind them.

His response automatic, Nick wrapped his right

arm around Cara, almost throwing her against the side of the building and then attempting to cover her body with his own. His ribs protested both the abruptness of the movement and the force with which he was pressing her against the wall.

By the time he'd retrieved his weapon from the shoulder holster under his blazer, he had recognized the unexpected sound for what it was. A garbage truck was emptying the motel's industrial Dumpster.

Adrenaline still pumping despite the knowledge that there was nothing to fear, he shoved the Glock into its holster as he eased back to look down into Cara's face. She was staring up at him, her eyes widened in shock. Still trusting that he hadn't completely lost his mind, in spite of what he'd just done, she had made no attempt to free herself.

And although Nick now knew he'd overreacted, he was in no hurry to release her. Her body was molded to his, her breasts rising and falling against his chest with the rapidity of her breathing. Since the first time he'd seen her at her father's funeral, the thought of holding her like this, every inch of that elegant body aligned to his, had been in the back of his mind.

Something in his face must have warned her that he was no longer worried about possible dangers. Her lips had been slightly parted as she looked up into his eyes. Seeing what was in them now, she closed her mouth and slipped her hands up between their bodies, her palms flattened against his chest, as if to push him away.

The right thing to do would be to take a step back, freeing her from a closeness she obviously wasn't comfortable with. Although he had always taken pride in his self-control, Nick found he was unable to make that move.

His head began to lower instead, slightly tilted to bring his mouth in line with hers. Rather than the protest he expected, her lips parted as if anticipating his kiss. And then her eyes closed—long, dark lashes falling against her colorless cheeks.

The pressure her palms had been exerting against his chest eased. Her fingers closed around the material of his shirt instead, using it to draw him closer to her. It was the only encouragement he needed.

His hands moved away from the wall on either side of her head to close around her back. His mouth found hers, still open, her lips soft and moist. His tongue pushed between them to be met immediately by hers. Together they began that slow dance of desire, which mirrored the one they both knew would happen eventually.

He pulled her closer, the heels of his hands at the small of her back, his fingers spread over the softness of her bottom. His arousal was suddenly full-blown, the frustrations of the past week forgotten. Everything forgotten except the woman he held in his arms.

The door to the room they were standing beside suddenly opened. Nick could hear the television blaring from inside, but that wasn't as startling as the sound of high-pitched voices.

Children.

Cara's hands unclenched, her palms again flattening against his chest to push him away. This time, driven by considerations other than what was happening between them, somehow he found the self-control to obey.

He stepped back, glancing to his left as he did. He'd been right. Two little girls, neither more than five or six years old, were eyeing them with open interest.

Just at that moment their mother came out of the room, pulling the door closed behind her as she adjusted the strap of the oversize purse on her shoulder. She never looked their way, shepherding her daughters toward the parking lot instead, one hand on each set of thin, childish shoulders. The little girls, seemingly fascinated by the kiss they'd interrupted, had to be prodded forward, their eyes still fastened on Nick and Cara.

He waited until they were out of earshot before he turned to look down on her face once more. Her mouth was closed, her gaze still following the threesome.

"Sorry."

Her eyes came up to meet his. "It was as much my fault as yours."

"Hardly."

"If you want to take the blame for that very public display, feel free, of course, but…I wasn't exactly pushing you away."

She hadn't been. At least not after that first tentative movement of her hands. Maybe he should consider that an invitation to continue the kiss once they got inside.

And maybe you need a reminder of exactly what you're doing right now. Which isn't trying to get Hiram Simonson's daughter into bed.

Take care of her, Polk had said, putting his finger on the crux of Nick's dilemma.

He was responsible for Cara being here. He had approached her because he'd believed he could use her expertise and easy access to get information from the FBI's files. In doing that, he'd gotten her involved in something that had almost gotten her killed, not once but twice.

No one knew better than he did what being that

close to death could do to a person's normal inhibitions. Every human instinct was to celebrate the fact that you were still alive. And people celebrated that in all sorts of ways, including physical intimacy.

"Maybe you should have been," he warned.

"What does that mean?"

"I've already told you my intentions. Maybe you need to think about whether or not you want to encourage them."

Her expression closed, the change subtle, but definite. Apparently she preferred not to be asked to make that kind of conscious choice. Of course, it was much easier just to drift into those situations.

For some reason, Nick had felt that he owed it to her not to let that happen. Or maybe that he owed it to her dead father.

The one thing he didn't want hanging over his head when this was over was guilt about having taken advantage of Cara. She needed time after learning the truth about her father's death to regain her equilibrium. Time to realize that eventually her life would go back to normal.

Whether she still wanted Nick to be a part of it then was something she would have to decide, but it wasn't fair to ask her to make that decision now. Not with everything that was going on.

"I'll take that under advisement," she said, her voice as tight as her face.

Nick nodded. He gestured that she should precede him to the room, and this time he made sure he did it without making the mistake of touching her.

NICK HAD ALLOWED CARA first crack at the bathroom again, despite the effects of the long day. He had popped three ibuprofen and stretched out on the bed while she'd showered and changed.

All he could think about was how her mouth had opened under the demand of his tongue and the feel of her body pressed against his. It was one thing to be noble and talk about choices. It was quite another to live with them. The image of her naked in the shower only a few feet away from where he lay didn't help.

When he came out of the bathroom more than an hour later, Cara was sitting on the foot of her bed. Her body was slightly hunched, her arms crossed over her chest as if she were cold.

When she raised her head to look at him, he knew exactly what was going on. Actually, he should have been expecting it.

"It doesn't do any good to think about it," he said.

"And how do you *not* think about it?"

"You focus on things you can do something about."

Duncan McGregor was dead. They had been too late. They could either embrace that failure and give up, or they could try to find the next name on the list before their enemy did.

That was something combat taught you. The dead are dead. There's nothing you can do for them. And the mission still exists.

"We don't seem to be having a lot of success in doing something about what's going on," she said. "And the closer we get to whoever this is, the more dangerous it becomes."

It was a fair assessment. Certainly not one he would argue with.

"There's nothing that says you have to be involved. You can get on the next plane out of Chattanooga in the morning."

"Is that what you're going to do?"

"I signed on to this knowing what I was getting into. You didn't. And that's my fault."

"I should have known. If you were right, they had already killed three people when you approached me."

"Knowing that intellectually isn't the same as almost getting blown to kingdom come."

She shivered, rubbing her right hand up and down her left arm. "Why didn't this bother me so much last night?"

"Last night you were partially insulated from its reality by adrenaline. And you were very grateful to be alive," he added softly.

"I still am."

"But now you've realized how close a thing it was."

"What can be that important?"

"I'm sorry?"

"Important enough to kill. And kill again."

"People kill for pocket change," he said, fighting the inclination to laugh at the naiveté she'd just expressed. "And the more you do it, the easier it becomes."

"And the better you get at it?"

"Probably," Nick admitted. "I meant what I said about going home."

He could tell by her eyes that she was considering it. After a moment, she shook her head.

"I kept thinking about him last night. Wondering if he knew what was going to happen to him. If he were terrified."

"McGregor?"

"My dad."

"Cara…"

He stopped because he didn't have any answers for

that kind of pain. And because he had wondered the same thing about his father.

"He was a good man. A good, brave man. I don't want to let them get away with it, Nick."

He nodded, his throat tight with the same determination. This had all begun because he hadn't wanted to believe his father's life had been so empty that he had chosen to end it.

Now that he knew that wasn't what had happened, he simply wanted revenge. And to prevent other good, brave men from dying because of something that had happened more than thirty years ago.

Chapter Twelve

"I probably should call Mom."

Nick had again risen first and made the coffee, although he had managed to sleep later this morning. She could tell from that and from the way he moved that his ribs weren't nearly as painful as they had been.

As soon as he'd realized she was awake and watching him, he had poured a second cup and brought it to the bed. He had even waited for her to rearrange her pillows behind her so she could lean back against the headboard to drink it.

She was a little surprised at the thoughtfulness of the gesture. It didn't seem in character, somehow. But then she was discovering that there were far more facets to Nick's character than she'd been aware of.

"What for?" he asked, watching her take her first careful sip of the hot liquid.

"Just to check on her. And to let her know that we're all right."

Miriam wouldn't have any way of knowing that they'd almost been blown up. She wouldn't necessarily be worried, but Cara found that she needed to hear her mom's voice. Maybe just to once more make contact with the stability that had always been at the center of her life.

She could tell from Nick's face that he was weighing whether or not talking to her mother was a good idea. Maybe he thought her call might inadvertently give away their location. Or far worse, somehow put Miriam in danger.

Of course, the people they were waging this war against had obviously expected them to be right here. The rigged cabin was proof of that. And surely whoever was behind the murders couldn't possibly be stupid enough to believe her mom was a threat to them.

Apparently Nick reached the same conclusion. "Be sure and ask her if she's remembered anything else that might help."

Cara nodded, setting down the coffee to pick up her cell phone from the bedside table. Yesterday she had been too busy or too distracted to think about charging it. She had realized only when she'd taken it out of her purse that it was dead, so she had plugged it in to the charger overnight.

The distant ringing seemed faint, but her aunt's voice when she answered was very clear. "Hello?"

"Aunt Margaret, it's Cara."

"How are you, dear?"

For a second or two, Cara actually considered saying something that might indicate how far out of her depth she felt. Anything approaching the truth would be lost on Margaret, however, and it would only trouble her mother.

"I'm fine. Is Mom around? I need to talk to her a minute."

"She's doing fine," Margaret said, obviously assuming that would be Cara's first concern.

And her mom's grief should have been, she acknowledged. It was just that so much had happened since her father's death that its tragedy seemed more distant than it really was.

"Much better than I ever expected," her aunt went on.

"That's good."

"Miriam's stronger than you'd think. She always looks so fragile you forget that core of steel."

Her aunt was right. Her mother's resilience was something Cara *had* forgotten. Seeing her tending to Nick the night of the hit-and-run should have reminded her.

"Here she is, dear. You take care now."

"I will. Thanks, Aunt Margaret."

"Hello?"

At the sound of that familiar voice, Cara's eyes burned. She blinked, controlling the unexpected tears.

"Just checking on you," she said.

For some reason she lifted her head and found that Nick had sat down on the edge of the other bed and was watching her. After the kiss they'd shared yesterday and the previous night's pronouncement, she found the intensity of his gaze disconcerting.

It made her conscious of how little she had on under the nightshirt. She resisted the urge to pull the sheet up over her breasts. She lowered her eyes instead, concentrating on the pattern of the bedspread that lay across her lap.

"I'm fine," Miriam said. "How are you?"

Despite all that was going on in their lives, the exchange was no different than most of their conversations through the years. So incredibly normal.

Cara decided there was no point in telling her

mother the truth about what had happened. Not unless she demanded more specifics.

"I'm okay. Nick wanted me to ask if you'd thought of any other names. Or of any incident Daddy might have mentioned from his tour."

"Did you find McGregor?"

There was no way to avoid answering that outright question. "Not in time," Cara admitted.

The silence on the other end of the line let her know that her mother understood what that meant.

"Oh, dear. Poor man."

Cara was relieved she didn't ask for details. If it hadn't been for their presence at the scene, McGregor's death would undoubtedly have been listed as an accident, just as her father's had been. There was something about the fact that it had happened in a fire that seemed to make McGregor's death even worse. More violent, somehow.

"That's why we were hoping you might have come up with something."

"I went back through your daddy's letters. It was something I wanted to do anyway, but... There really doesn't seem to be anything there that might be helpful."

It was the same conclusion Cara had come to during the long night she'd spent reading them. "I know. Thanks for trying though."

"I'm just sorry that I can't be any more help. You would think that after living with him all these years, I'd know more about those months than I do."

"Daddy didn't want you to know."

"I should have asked. I should have tried."

"Don't do this, Mom. There's no way you could have known that any of that might have been important. There's no way anyone could have known."

"It's like when I thought he'd been drinking. I just keep wondering why this was happening."

"That's what Nick is trying to find out," Cara soothed, raising her eyes to look at him again. He was still focused on the conversation, although it had become personal rather than relating to the questions he needed answers for.

"It's hard to put it out of my mind."

"I know," Cara said softly, remembering the images of her father's last moments that had troubled her last night.

"Oh," her mom said, her tone changing suddenly, maybe deliberately, "before I forget… When I checked the machine at home, there was a message for you. Someone from your company I think. I tried to call your cell phone to tell you about it, but I couldn't get you."

Her mother never left messages. She had an aversion to talking to recorders or voice-mail systems.

"I forgot to charge it. Do you remember who called?"

Cara wasn't particularly surprised that her employer was trying to reach her. They were in a crucial stage of the project, some important parts of it her responsibility. She *was* surprised, however, that, even if they couldn't have reached her on the cell, they would have called her parents' number. It seemed an unnecessary invasion of her mother's grief.

When Cara had received the news of her father's death, she hadn't been sure how long she would be gone. Her immediate supervisor, Jack Hammond, had told her to take as much time as she needed, but maybe something critical to the success of the project had come up in the meantime.

"Ainsworth," her mother said. "I wrote it down because it didn't sound familiar."

It didn't sound familiar to Cara, either. She was almost positive that there was no one working on the FBI project with that name. Orvid was a big company, however, and it could be that someone at headquarters had been referred to her. Maybe Jack had routed the call through.

"Do you have his number?"

As her mother read it off, Cara realized that it was a D.C. number. Not someone from corporate then.

"And you're sure it was someone with the company."

There was a small hesitation. "He asked you to call him. He said *something* about Orvid. I guess I assumed he was someone with the company."

"It doesn't matter. I just didn't recognize the name."

"Are you going back to Washington?"

Cara supposed that was up to Nick, but it seemed they had again reached a dead end. There was nothing of any use to them in the burned-out shell of McGregor's cabin. Whatever records or mementos he might have kept from his service in Vietnam were now destroyed.

"I don't know," Cara said, focusing on Nick's face again. "I'll have to let you know."

"I'm thinking about going back home," her mother said. "No sense in trying to run away from the fact that your father's gone."

"And there's no sense in being at home by yourself, either. Not when you don't have to."

"Then you aren't coming back?"

There was a wistful note to her mother's voice, but obviously she knew the answer. The message she'd

found on her phone yesterday would only have confirmed what she was already well aware of. Her
daughter's professional life was a demanding one.

"Just as soon as I can get another few days off,"
Cara promised. "The project's at a critical stage right
now. Why don't you spend a few more days with Aunt
Margaret and then plan to come and stay with me for
a while?"

Because the work they were doing for the Bureau
would take several months, Cara had rented an apartment inside the Beltway. Although it was only one
bedroom, there was a sleeper sofa.

"I'll think about it," her mother said. "I always
sleep better in my own bed."

"Maybe you shouldn't go home until this is
over…" Cara began and then hesitated. Before she
could decide how much to say about the possibility
that her mother might be in danger, Nick reached for
the phone.

"Let me talk to her."

Maybe that kind of warning would be better coming from him. It was always difficult to assume a
parental role with one's own parent. And that wasn't
a position Cara had ever wanted, in any case.

She laid her cell onto Nick's outstretched palm. As
she did, her fingers made an unintentional contact
with his hand. With the touch, a frisson of sexual
awareness moved through her lower body. She
couldn't believe he hadn't felt the spark of electrical
current that had seemed to arc between them, but his
face remained impassive as he brought the phone up
to his ear.

"Miriam? Nick Morelli."

He listened a moment, his dark eyes holding on

Cara's face. She couldn't imagine what her mother might be saying to him.

"Much better, thanks."

Ribs. A medical question. The slight sense of apprehension she'd felt eased as she continued to listen.

"I'm not sure it's a good idea for you to go back home until we understand what's going on."

Another silence.

"Not really. I just don't like to operate in the dark, and that's essentially what we're doing. I'd feel better, and I know Cara would, if we knew you were somewhere safe."

A shorter pause this time.

"A few days at the most."

Whatever her mother said in response to that caused the subtle movement at the corner of Nick's mouth again. The amusement was mirrored in his dark eyes.

"I will. I promise. That isn't anything you need to worry about. Just stay where you are until you hear from me."

She probably would, Cara thought. Although her own arguments had had little or no effect on her mother, Nick seemed confident that he'd talked her into remaining at her sister's.

Maybe it was a generational thing, as she'd originally surmised. Or maybe her mother simply responded to Nick's air of confidence. Just as *she* always did, Cara acknowledged.

She deferred to his expertise because she wasn't stupid. Nick knew what he was doing, and she didn't have a clue. Apparently he had convinced her mother of his competence, as well.

She looked up in time to see Nick turn off the phone. "What did she say?"

"I think she'll stay there. For the time being at least."

"I meant what did she say that amused you?"

"She told me to keep an eye on you."

"And that made you smile?"

Smile was too strong a word for that increasingly familiar, one-sided tilt of his lips, but she couldn't think of anything else to call it.

"Because it was such an unnecessary reminder."

"Unnecessary?" Again her heart rate accelerated, although there was more than one possible interpretation of what he'd just said.

Nick didn't rise to the bait she offered. If she had wanted to hear him say he didn't find it difficult to keep his eyes on her, she was destined to be disappointed.

"They want you to come back to Washington?" he asked instead.

"I can't be sure until I talk to whoever this is, but...given the situation, I wouldn't be surprised. After all, they do pay my salary."

A very nice one, too. And this was the largest contract Orvid had ever landed. The company had a right to expect her to pull her share of the load.

"I'm sorry if you think I'm running out on you," she offered, "but I don't know what else I can do to help."

"Call them and see what they want. We can talk about what comes next after you know for sure."

She nodded, but there was really no other reason anyone would be calling her only a few days after her father's funeral. Obviously this was something urgent, she thought as she punched in the number her mother had given her.

"Richard Ainsworth's office."

"This is Cara Simonson. I'm returning Mr. Ainsworth's call."

"Of course, Ms. Simonson. Mr. Ainsworth is out of the office right now, but I can have him call you back as soon as he gets in, or, if you'd prefer, you can leave a message."

"Since I'm not sure what he called me about, it might be better if you have him get in touch with me again," Cara said.

She gave her cell phone number, and then, before the secretary could disconnect, she asked the question that had been troubling her since her mother had told her about the message.

"And exactly how is Mr. Ainsworth connected to Orvid?"

"Orvid?" the secretary repeated, her voice conveying what sounded like genuine puzzlement. "I'm afraid I'm not familiar with the term."

Obviously if his secretary wasn't familiar with the company name, then Ainsworth wasn't with corporate.

"I understood Mr. Ainsworth's call was in regards to a project we're involved in. If he's not with Orvid…"

Deliberately Cara left the sentence hanging, and just as she had hoped, the secretary filled in the information she had been looking for.

"Mr. Ainsworth is an executive assistant director of the Federal Bureau of Investigation, Ms. Simonson. Does that help?"

"IF THIS WERE ABOUT the project, they wouldn't be calling me directly," Cara said. "Believe me, I'm not that important. They'd go through Jack Hammond or one of the people at corporate."

"So why else would the FBI be trying to get in touch with you?" Nick asked reasonably.

The only contact she'd had with the Bureau that hadn't involved the work Orvid was doing to revamp the outdated computer system was when she had approached one of their agents about Don Crawford's death. That didn't seem an adequate reason for the assistant executive director to call her.

"I don't know. The only thing I can think of is my question about Crawford's death. And I deliberately kept that low-key. The agent I talked to, whose name is Burke Raymond by the way, didn't seem to think anything at all about my asking. I can't imagine how or why it would have reached the ears of someone like Ainsworth."

"How much information did you give Raymond when you made that call?"

"None, really. I asked him if he could find out if there had been any suspicion of foul play in Crawford's death."

"And he didn't ask you any questions?"

"He asked why I thought there might be. I told him that a friend who knew Crawford thought his death was strange. Believe me, it was all very casual. Almost…gossipy."

She didn't like the word, but she couldn't think of another that conveyed the tone she had tried to strike. As if she were simply curious about something she'd heard.

"He bought it?"

"He seemed to. He called me back and said that as far as the Bureau was concerned Crawford's death was from natural causes. A massive coronary."

"And that's when you asked him about drugs that might mimic a heart attack?"

She had forgotten she'd told Nick that. But he was right. She had asked that question.

"Only after he said that they'd done a tox screen because of Crawford's age and nothing unusual had shown up."

"Most of the drugs used to produce a 'coronary' wouldn't show up. Not unless you were looking for them specifically. I doubt the Bureau did."

That was the same thing Nick had told her before. Crawford's death could have been arranged, and unless the FBI had reason to be suspicious, they would never discover it.

"You think that's what this is about? They want to know why I was inquiring about Crawford's death?"

"I don't know. You could call your boss and see if there's anything going on with the project that might make someone like Ainsworth want to talk to you."

"If I do that, he'll want to know when I'm coming back to work."

Nick let the implied question lie between them for a few seconds. Cara found that in spite of knowing that she was in way over her head, she wanted him to suggest that she shouldn't do that yet. When he didn't, her disappointment was unexpectedly sharp.

"And you don't know the answer to that?" he asked.

"I don't know what comes next. We seem to have run out of options."

"What we've run out of is information."

"So what do we do about it?"

"Maybe go see if Mr. Ainsworth will give us a fresh supply."

Chapter Thirteen

Washington, D.C.

They picked Nick's car up from long-term parking at the airport in D.C. Despite his warning that they were no longer just the hunters, but also the hunted, Cara was surprised at the thoroughness with which he examined the Jeep Cherokee.

Although their appointment at the FBI was in little more than an hour, Nick took time to check under both the chassis and the hood. When he was finally satisfied there were no explosives rigged to go off as he started the engine, he opened the passenger side door, shifting a briefcase and a stack of file folders from the seat into the back to give her a place to sit.

"Sorry. I'm afraid my car has become an extension of my office."

"That's okay. Mine would be the same way if I had one."

"The house will be almost as bad. It's the maid's year off."

There seemed only one possible interpretation of that. "Is that where we're going after we meet with Ainsworth? To your house?"

"I've probably got better security."

The need for security had become the new reality in her life. It was still difficult for her to fathom that someone had tried to kill her twice. Although that was clearly because of her association with Nick, once that connection had been established, he apparently felt that she—and maybe even her mother—would be a target.

"Unless you think your place would be better for some reason?" Nick asked as he backed the car out of its parking space.

A quick mental picture of the apartment she'd rented, chosen for its proximity to her work rather than its spaciousness, made that decision a no-brainer. Wherever Nick lived, it would surely have more space. And therefore less forced intimacy. Of course, for two people who had just spent the last couple of nights sharing a motel room…

"No, that's fine," she said quickly, banishing the image of Nick stretched out on that double bed from her head. "Whatever you think is best."

He's the expert, she reminded herself. The one who knows what he's doing. *Dear God, I hope so.*

"And I need to touch base with my boss," Nick said. "He may have turned up something useful."

"The private investigator?"

Even in profile she could see that movement at the corner of his mouth. "You could call him that."

"What do *you* call him?"

"Griff," he said, the lift of his lips more pronounced. "And a friend."

"He's working on this?"

"When I asked him to vouch for me with Sheriff Polk, I had to explain what was going on. He's going to try to get some additional information about the men on the list through his contacts."

"Friends in high places," she said softly, remembering Sheriff Polk's words.

Something about her tone made Nick glance at her before he turned his eyes back to the afternoon traffic. "He was my superior at the Agency."

"At the CIA."

He nodded, but he didn't look at her again.

"So...his connections are through them."

Another nod.

"Does he know anything about Ainsworth?"

"I haven't had a chance to ask him. I wanted to see what Ainsworth has to say first. Get a feel for whether or not he might be an ally."

"And if you get the feeling that he's not?"

"He may still be useful. Sometimes what people choose to hide can be as revealing as what they choose to share."

"And what will we choose to share with him?"

"Everything we know and most of what we suspect," Nick said. "We need Ainsworth a lot more than he needs us."

"THANK YOU FOR coming in, Ms. Simonson."

"I wasn't sure I had a choice."

Cara's voice sounded as cool and poised as she looked. The plainly cut navy-blue suit she wore with a white silk shirt seemed both professional and incredibly sexy. He would probably think that about anything she put on, Nick acknowledged.

"Of course you had a choice," the assistant executive director said, smiling at her. Judging by Ainsworth's eyes, the outfit seemed to be having the same effect on him. "But I appreciate your responding so quickly to my request."

He turned to look at Nick, one brow cocked questioningly. He was obviously waiting for an explanation of why he had accompanied Cara to this meeting. She gave him the one she and Nick had agreed on during the drive from the airport to the FBI building.

"This is an associate of mine, Nick Morelli. I've asked him to sit in on our meeting. I hope that's all right."

Ainsworth held his hand out to Nick across the polished surface of his desk. "Do *I* have a choice?" he asked, repeating her opening phrase with a hint of amusement in his deep voice.

"Not really," Nick said easily.

Ainsworth's grip was firm, but his palm felt soft and a little fleshy. If he had been a field agent at one time, apparently he no longer took advantage of the Bureau's excellent training facilities.

"Then won't you *both* have a seat? Ms. Simonson." Ainsworth indicated the leather armchair situated directly across the desk from his. "And Mr. Morelli." This time he gestured toward a straight-backed chair that sat beside a long table under the row of windows.

Nick retrieved it instead, putting it down beside Cara's. He was pretty sure that wasn't what the assistant executive director had in mind, but he wasn't about to play by rules someone else had devised. Not at this stage of the game.

"As I mentioned during my second call," Ainsworth began, ignoring Nick's small act of defiance, "I wanted to talk to you about your inquiry concerning Special Agent Don Crawford. Do you mind telling me why you questioned the circumstances surrounding his death?"

This, too, was something they had prepared for. If they were going to get any useful information out of the FBI, they would need to give them something in exchange, something that might prime the pump.

"Because I suggested she should," Nick said.

Ainsworth shifted his attention to Nick. "And why was that?"

"I don't believe Crawford died of a heart attack."

"You knew Agent Crawford?"

"No."

"Then forgive me, but…I'm still not sure why you have questions about his death."

"Because he made an appointment with my father the day before he died."

"Your father?" Ainsworth's tone clearly conveyed his skepticism about the relevance of that comment.

"Vincent Morelli."

Although Nick had been watching the assistant executive director carefully, he could detect no reaction to his father's name. Of course, it could just as easily be that Ainsworth had been expecting to hear it as that he'd never heard it before.

"And this…appointment made you suspicious of Agent Crawford's death?"

"Since my father died the day before he was supposed to keep it, yes, it did."

There was a small silence as Ainsworth appeared to digest that information. "Do you know what their meeting was about?"

"I know that whatever it was got them both killed."

Another beat of silence.

"How did your father die, Mr. Morelli?"

"According to the coroner he put his service revolver in his mouth and pulled the trigger."

"Obviously you don't believe that."

"My father wasn't the kind of man who would commit suicide. I thought that when they first called me to tell me he was dead. And then I found Crawford's message on his machine."

"With all due respect to your grief—"

"And beside his chair, a list of names and some photographs."

Ainsworth's lips pursed slightly, but he didn't pose another question. Apparently he had decided to let Nick tell this in his own way. Which was fine by him. It would save time in the long run.

"The photos were taken during my father's service in Vietnam. That was something he never talked about, so I wondered why he had those pictures out and beside his chair when he died. And I also wondered why he was meeting with an FBI agent."

"A meeting you say Crawford arranged?"

That was another piece of the puzzle Nick still didn't have an answer for. Had Crawford initiated contact, causing his dad to dig out those old photographs, or had his father's call to the Bureau come first?

"I don't know which of them arranged it. I believe that information would be in Agent Crawford's files. If so, it might be helpful."

"Helpful in what?"

"In finding out who murdered my father. And Cara's father, Hiram Simonson. A man named Duncan McGregor in Tennessee. And your agent, of course."

"That's quite a string of accusations." Again Ainsworth sounded almost amused. "If you have some basis for making them, other than a missed appointment and some photographs, I'd be interested in hearing it."

"Both Simonson and McGregor were on the list of names I found beside my father's chair. Both of them died within a few days of my father's supposed suicide. *And* within a few days of Crawford's heart attack. It's obvious there's a connection."

"You buy into that?" Ainsworth had addressed this question to Cara.

"I didn't. Not at first. Not until I found out certain details about my father's accident that made me doubt the theory the police had advanced as to cause of death."

"Which were?"

"That he got drunk and drove his car over an embankment. And before you offer 'all due respect' to *my* grief, Mr. Ainsworth, let me assure you that, unlike Nick, I was perfectly willing to believe that's how my father died. Until I started asking the questions Nick suggested and found that none of the answers I was given added up. The position of the seat in the car that night was wrong for my father's height. The bottle they'd put in the car wasn't a brand he would ever drink. I know you're thinking those are minor points on which to build an accusation of murder, but added to Mr. Morelli's and Agent Crawford's deaths and to the fact that my father's name was on the list Nick found, it seemed a compelling case to me."

Again there was another silence as the executive assistant director seemed to consider what Cara had just said. Despite her initial doubts, Nick thought she had presented the evidence on her father's death both concisely and coherently. It would be difficult to argue with the associations she'd made.

"You mentioned a third name."

"Duncan McGregor," Nick said. "The names on

my father's list were either first names or nicknames, most of them impossible to identify. I was able to obtain a roster of all the men who served in the battalion during the time around my father's tour of duty. We've been trying to match someone from it to the list my father composed. We thought that a man with a name like Duncan McGregor might possibly have been called Scottie. Apparently we were right, but too late in drawing that conclusion. By the time we got to McGregor, someone had filled his cabin with gas and rigged it to explode when the door was opened."

"With him inside?"

"I'm afraid so. The fire marshal concluded it was an obvious case of arson, so although we can't prove he was the Scottie on my dad's list, it *can* be verified that someone murdered McGregor. And that he served at the same time as my father and in the same company."

"When the coincidences continue to pile up, one after another, it becomes harder and harder to ignore them," Cara said, repeating the argument Nick and her mother had used to convince her. "But frankly, we've reached a dead end on the other names on the list. We can't identify any of them. That's why, when you left a message for me, we decided to appeal to you for help in finding those men."

"I'm flattered that you have such faith in my abilities, Ms. Simonson," Ainsworth said, "but I'm not sure how you expect me to pull that off. Not if you're unable to match any of them against the battalion roster."

"A good place to start would be Crawford's case files," Nick suggested. "If we knew what he and my father intended to talk about at their meeting, maybe we could make those identifications in some other way."

"Such as?"

"If there was a specific incident Crawford had wanted to ask my father about. Maybe something those people on his list knew about."

"Related to Vietnam?"

"That's my best guess, given the photographs he'd pulled and the fact that the three men who are dead all served there with him," Nick said.

"The Bureau has sometimes been accused of being mired in the past, but I'm not sure why you think one of our agents would be interested in something that happened…what? Thirty years ago?"

"Closer to thirty-five. It had to have occurred while these people were there."

"Something criminal?"

"I don't know," Nick admitted, and then hit the point he wanted to make again, "but Crawford might have."

"The statute of limitations would have run out a long time ago on most of the illegal activities, like drug-running and arms sales, associated with that period."

"But not on others," Nick reminded him. "Not on treason. Or murder. We can't know what Crawford was investigating until you have someone look into his files."

"You're aware, of course, that those are classified."

"I'm not asking you to let us see them. I'm asking you to investigate what he was working on. Maybe if we knew that, we could identify the other names on the list. And possibly get to them before somebody arranges it so there are no more witnesses at all to whatever Crawford was interested in."

"Do you think he'll do it?" Cara asked as soon as the door to the executive assistant director's office had closed behind them.

Ainsworth had made no promises. He had copied

down the remaining names on Nick's list and asked where he could reach them, but he hadn't agreed to search Crawford's files. Or to do anything else.

"He may already have."

"Are you saying he *knows* what Crawford was working on?"

"Why else would he call you in? I don't buy the idea that he was simply curious about your request."

"Maybe I should call the agent I asked about Crawford and see if he knows what's going on."

"Except he's the only one who could have told the Bureau you were making inquiries."

"I didn't ask him to keep that in confidence. At the time, because I wasn't convinced there was anything to your theory, I assumed no one would be particularly interested."

"That's always another possibility," Nick said.

"What? I don't understand."

"Maybe Ainsworth doesn't know what Crawford was working on. Maybe what he knows is that he didn't have a heart attack."

"So he called me in to see how I'd come by that information?"

"Maybe he was hoping you'd give them a place to start."

"If he was, that doesn't bode well for our request," Cara said. "If they thought there was something suspicious about Crawford's death, then they would already have been all over those files. Maybe there really is nothing there."

"Or maybe Ainsworth wanted to know how much we knew. Maybe he was on a fishing expedition, too."

"So who won the trophy?" Cara asked.

"I don't think we'll know that until he calls us back."

Chapter Fourteen

Watching in the rearview mirror to make sure they weren't being followed, Nick negotiated an exit off the interstate that led to an exclusive suburb of the capital. The upscale area didn't fit with Cara's preconceived idea of where he might live. Of course, it had been that way almost from the moment she'd met him. As soon as she thought she had him figured out, he did something that surprised her.

And that was exactly the reaction she had as he pulled the Jeep up before a set of huge, wrought-iron gates flanked by security cameras. He opened them with a remote on his key ring and then drove through them and onto the grounds of what could only be described as an estate. The long drive meandered between tall oaks and poplars, whose leaves were just beginning to be tinged with red and gold, to end at a Tudor-style mansion spread out over the top of a low hill.

"Don't get your hopes up," Nick said, that slight lift back at the corner of his mouth. "This one isn't mine. I live in what used to be referred to around here as the servants' quarters."

He drove past the circular drive and toward the rear

of the mansion. A small guesthouse, built of the same material as the main house, sat under a stand of oaks. Beyond it, within walking distance, were neatly maintained stables and padlocks, their fences all of the same weathered cedar from which the two houses had been constructed.

"Nice," she said.

Understatement.

"It belongs to a relative of a friend. The guesthouse was sitting empty, so..."

Nick let the sentence trail as he pulled up to the brick sidewalk leading to what he'd called the servants' quarters. Either there was nothing more to the story of how he'd come to be living here or he didn't want to explain any further. In either case, it seemed an incredibly generous gesture on the part of his friend.

And he had obviously been right about the security. There seemed little chance the people who'd set off that explosion in Tennessee would find their way here. If they did, they'd have a hard time getting past the security fence that protected the main house.

Nick grabbed both bags from the back of the Jeep before he came around to open her door. He set his suitcase down and offered his hand to help her out of the car. After the flight and the drive from the airport, it felt good to stand up and stretch her legs.

"Anybody at home?" she asked, looking at the mansion behind them. When she turned back to him, she found that Nick was bending inside the car to retrieve his gun from the glove box.

"The man who lives there is visiting his goddaughter right now." His voice was slightly muffled by his position.

The man who lives there...

That made it sound as if someone lived in that huge place all alone. Of course, whatever the arrangements were, they were none of her business. Not even the one that had allowed Nick to occupy the guesthouse.

As she turned to follow him up the brick walkway, some of the unease she'd been feeling about staying with him began to dissipate. As old-fashioned as it might seem, she was relieved that there would be no one else on the grounds.

Although the sexual tension between her and Nick seemed to increase with every hour they spent together, they weren't lovers. Nowhere close. But that was something anyone who saw him carrying her suitcase into his house would certainly have assumed.

She wasn't sure why that assumption would make her uncomfortable. It wasn't as if she'd never been involved with a man.

Just never with one like Nick Morelli...

Nick had stopped at the front door of the guesthouse, his key in his hand. He hesitated, seeming reluctant to insert it into the lock.

And why wouldn't he be? she thought, remembering, as she knew he must be, the explosion and fire at the cabin.

"Come on," he said, slipping his weapon out of the waistband of his khaki slacks where he'd shoved it after retrieving it from the Jeep.

"We're leaving?"

She could see nothing about the entranceway that might have made him suspicious. Actually, she would have a hard time imagining a more peaceful setting.

"I think we'll go in through the back."

She wanted to remind him that that was exactly what they'd done at McGregor's. *And that's sheer paranoia,* she told herself, feeling as if she were being disloyal. *Just because Nick is careful doesn't mean there's anything to worry about.*

If they're *really* trying to kill you, it isn't paranoia. Just as that old saying—no longer the least bit amusing—popped into her head, Nick stepped off the low stoop. Before she could follow him, part of the wooden door they'd been standing in front of seemed to explode outward.

There was no noise, but she could feel splinters strike her cheek. She closed her eyes instinctively, protecting them from the stinging burst of fragments.

Before she had time to open them again, she heard the high-pitched crack of a gun. Obviously the one that had fired the bullet that had struck the door between them. Even to her untutored ears, it was clear the shot had come from the woods to their left.

That was all she had time to figure out before Nick grabbed her arm to jerk her down. The angle at which the Jeep was parked at the end of the walk afforded some protection. Nick's gun, already cradled in his hand, should supply even more. Still, with the hole in the door behind her as a reminder of how close a thing it had been, Cara felt too exposed.

"Shouldn't we get inside?"

"I'm not sure that isn't what they want us to do. That shot came *after* I stepped away from the door."

Intended to force them to do exactly what she'd just suggested? Had they set a trap inside this house, just as they had in Tennessee?

"Stay here," Nick ordered abruptly.

Adrenaline surging, she nodded unthinkingly. Despite his command, she was shocked when he began a crouching run toward the protection of the Jeep.

She actually reached for him, trying to prevent him from leaving, but he'd been moving too quickly. Her hand grasped only air.

Hunched down beside the foundation plantings that surrounded the guesthouse, she lifted her eyes to the woods that lay beyond the drive. They were too dense and distant to allow her to see anything of their assailant. Which meant he must be using a rifle with a scope, she realized.

Given the season, no matter how long he'd been up, there was little danger his stakeout would be challenged. If anyone had come upon him, he could simply pretend to be another hunter out for a day in the woods.

Or maybe, as Nick had hypothesized before, their assailant had known exactly when they would arrive in the D.C. area. Exactly when their plane had set down. And it wouldn't be hard to figure out the two possible locations where they might be headed.

My place or yours? Nick had obviously chosen the wrong one, she thought, glancing back at him.

She realized that he had been turned toward her, his hand outstretched, while she'd been considering the woods where the shooter was hidden. Had he been motioning that she should leave her position to join him at his?

If Nick was right about the possibility of the guesthouse being booby-trapped, then the Jeep offered the only way out of this situation. The scope on his rifle gave their assailant an unfair advantage, effectively pinning Nick down behind the vehicle.

Her eyes considered the stretch of browning grass

between them. The lawn had seemed charmingly pocket-size when she'd first seen it. Now, however...

She looked back at Nick, but his attention was directed toward that expanse of forest from where the shot had come. Obviously he was prepared to provide cover for her to join him.

She closed her eyes, trying not to think about whoever was waiting up in those woods. Trying not to imagine what a bullet that could gouge a hole in a solid wood door would do to a human body. Trying not to think about anything but her father and what these bastards had done to him.

Her eyes opened with the force of that memory. She knew that Nick wouldn't intentionally use her as bait, but her run across that stretch of grass could offer such a tempting target that their assailant might give up his cover, if only momentarily, and allow Nick to get off a shot.

So far she hadn't made any significant contribution to this effort. Maybe it was time she did.

Without allowing herself to think any more about what she had to do, she gathered the muscles in her calves and thighs. Then she pushed off the ground with her right hand, running as hard as she could for the Jeep.

She had forgotten about the low crouch Nick had assumed when he'd made his move. It was only when she felt a bullet brush past her that she bent. The crack of sound that followed a fraction of a second later urged her even lower.

She tried to focus on Nick as she ran. Everything seemed to be happening in slow motion. The movement of her legs. The pump of blood through her veins. Nick's body rising from behind the protective shield of the automobile, arms extended in front of him, his left hand cupped under the right, which held his gun.

On some level she was aware that he had returned fire. The sound of a second shot followed the first so closely that for a moment she thought it was an echo.

Except the bullet ricocheted off the tree in front of her, tearing off a chunk of bark. She flinched as it flew by a few inches to her right.

Nick fired again, never moving from the shooter's stance he'd assumed, despite the gunshots from the woods. By the time the noise of his second round had died away, she'd reached the Jeep.

Panting, she fell to her knees against the rear tire, still warm from its recent contact with the interstate. The hot-rubber scent of it was almost nauseating.

It was also comforting, however, because it meant she was safe. For the moment at least.

Despite her fear, she had done what she'd hoped she would. She had drawn the shooter out and given Nick a chance at him. She didn't know if he'd been successful. All she knew was that *she* had.

Somewhere inside her, despite the sickness and the stone-cold fear that had threatened to paralyze her as she'd crouched beside the guesthouse, there was a feeling of exhilaration. Of bone-deep satisfaction. Hers had been a puny blow at an unseen enemy, but from somewhere she had found the courage to strike it.

"What the hell did you think you were doing?"

She opened her eyes to find Nick squatting in front of her. His dark eyes were coldly furious, his face rigid. With the hand that wasn't wrapped around the butt of his gun, he grabbed her chin, forcing her head up.

She opened her mouth to protest. And then, before she could blurt out the truth, she realized that whatever he had wanted her to do when he'd looked back at her and gestured, obviously it hadn't been this.

She'd been congratulating herself on finally making some worthwhile contribution. Instead she had apparently just made a fool of herself. And had put both of them into danger at the same time.

"I'm sorry," she began, her breath still coming unevenly so that the words were staccato and broken. "I thought—"

"You thought what?"

She closed her mouth, swallowing against the painful dryness in her throat. "I thought you wanted me to do that."

"To almost get yourself killed? Why the *hell* would I want that?"

"I thought—"

Again she hesitated, feeling more like an idiot than she ever had in her life. She had always been the one at the head of the class. The one who knew exactly what she was supposed to do and did it successfully.

Nick's hold on her chin suddenly tightened. She thought he was again demanding an explanation. When she opened her mouth to try to give him one, he lowered his head, putting his lips over hers.

They were cold, and she was shocked to find that they were trembling as they closed roughly over hers. The kiss was deep and hard, almost abrupt. Expressing the same anger his voice had held.

He raised his head only enough to allow his lips to move. "Don't you *ever* do anything like that again. You hear me?"

She nodded, knowing that he was close enough to

feel the movement. He lowered his head again. This time the kiss was a caress, slow and thorough. Exactly what a kiss should be. Exactly what it should feel like.

She lifted her hand to touch his cheek. His skin was warm beneath the tips of her shaking fingers. After a moment he turned his head, his mouth brushing against them.

"Promise me."

The words were obviously a demand, but his fury seemed to have disappeared.

She nodded again.

"God, when I saw you get up and start over here—"

His fingers touched the hand that still rested against his face. He turned it over, pressing a kiss into the palm. He took a breath, seeming to gather control.

"Come on."

He released her to reach up and open the door to the back seat. He swept the stuff he'd put there at the airport onto the floor.

"Get in. And stay down."

"What about our bags?"

"Unless you have something in yours that you can't live without…"

Something you can't live without. That put it all into perspective.

"Good," he said, as if she had answered him. "Now get in. And keep your head down."

"What are you going to do?"

If he were planning to go after the man in the woods, she wasn't about to be left alone down here, wondering what was happening. Maybe her contribution to this effort had been nothing short of suicidal, but that didn't mean she was now going to sit back and let Nick put himself at further risk.

"I'm going to get behind the wheel and get us the hell out of here. Unless you've got any objections?"

Chapter Fifteen

She was still shaking when Nick stopped the car. Remembering his instructions, she didn't raise her head, not even when he cut off the engine and got out, slamming the door behind him. She lay on the back seat, reduced to waiting for whatever came next.

That was what she hated the most about all this. That lack of control. As if she and Nick were pawns in some game they didn't fully understand.

She jumped when the door opened, looking up automatically. Nick was standing outside, his eyes not on her, but scanning the area around the Jeep.

"Come on."

The command was almost as brusque as those he'd given her back at the guesthouse. Maybe he was still angry, but by now she had regained some of her shattered self-esteem.

"Where are we?"

Her question brought his attention—and his gaze—back to her. "On the busiest street corner I could find on short notice."

His eyes shifted once more as he stepped back and held up his hand, motioning broadly toward himself.

It wasn't until a taxi pulled up beside the Jeep that she understood the gesture.

"We're leaving the car?" she asked, starting to scramble out.

"It's one of the ways they might be tracking our movements," he said, opening the back door of the cab for her to crawl into.

"I don't understand."

"Locator beacon," he said as he followed her into the back seat.

Locator beacon? The words made no sense, until she suddenly realized what he must mean.

"You think there's a radio transmitter attached to your *car?*"

"It sat unattended at the airport for over a week. Plenty of time for anyone who was looking for it to find it."

Which was why, of course, he had checked it so carefully. Apparently he wasn't confident that he would be able to spot something as small as a locator.

"You think that's how they knew we were at the guesthouse?"

Being tracked by a radio transmitter sounded like something out of a James Bond movie. Of course, for a former CIA operative, thinking that way was probably routine.

Nick shook his head. "That ambush had to have been set up in advance. But someone who was willing to go to all that trouble might also be willing to go to a little extra effort in order to track our movements. Just in case we didn't show up where they expected us."

"So…where are we going?"

"Where they *don't* expect us," Nick said, leaning forward to give his instructions to the driver.

THE ELEGANT OLD Washington hotel, surrounded by shade trees and flower beds, had always been one of his favorites. There had even been a room available in the older section, where both the doors and walls were thick.

As soon as they were inside it, Nick flipped on the night latch and then slipped the safety chain into its slot. When he turned around, he found Cara watching him, her eyes expressing something that looked like apprehension. Maybe, as he was right now, she was remembering the promise he'd made.

When I make love to you, it won't be in some cheap motel. And I won't be moving like some stove-up rodeo hotshot.

Both of the conditions he'd set had been met. There was nothing cheap about this place, and he hadn't even thought about his ribs during the last twenty-four hours. Granted, that was as much because there had been too many other things to think of as because they were completely healed. They weren't, but he also knew they were no longer a hindrance to anything he wanted to do.

And looking at her now, he admitted there was almost nothing he'd rather do than make love to Cara. Except that he needed to be thinking about keeping her alive rather than taking her to bed.

"I have to make a phone call," he said.

Her eyes widened slightly. "Do you want me to wait in the bathroom?"

He shook his head. "There's nothing I'm going to say that you can't hear. Actually, you probably should hear it."

She nodded, moving away from the desk where the phone sat. She walked over and sat down on the end of the bed, crossing her arms over her chest, her right hand running up and down her left arm. It was the same hunched, protective posture she had assumed after the explosion.

She obviously needed reassurance that, despite what had happened today, she was safe. And she was. As safe as he could make her right now.

Somehow after letting her end up in the middle of an ambush, it didn't seem as if it would be very comforting to tell her that. Or very believable.

He walked over and picked up the phone instead, punching in the number of the Phoenix D.C. office. Griff's secretary routed the call through immediately.

"Cabot."

Just hearing the deep voice of the Phoenix head eased some of the "us against the world" feeling that had been growing during the last couple of days. Although Nick was an acknowledged loner, he had been part of a team of highly experienced operatives for years. And he had finally admitted it was time to call on all the resources of the Phoenix.

He had known from the first that those were his for the asking. He had just never acquired the habit of seeking help for personal problems. If he had been the only one involved in this, he might still be resisting making this second call for help.

"We just got ambushed at Mr. Gardner's place," he said without preamble. Griff knew enough about what was going on to be able to put the information into perspective. "Someone in the woods on the eastern ridge that overlooks the grounds."

"Anyone hurt?"

Cabot's question was calm, his voice unruffled, despite the fact that Nick had just informed him about a sniper on property belonging to his wife's grandfather. Although Gardner was visiting his goddaughter Raine at the Gulf, the breach in the estate's security would be of immediate concern to Cabot. Particularly because the old man had suffered a brutal beating during the last high-profile case the Phoenix agency had broken.

"We're fine, but it's obvious they know a lot more about us than I thought they did when I called you from Tennessee."

"And apparently they're more proficient than *either* of us gave them credit for," Griff said.

After the attack on Gardner, Cabot had beefed up security around the old man's house. Although it hadn't been presented to Gardner in that light, Cabot's concerns for his safety had prompted Nick's move into the guesthouse as an additional protective measure. If Claire's grandfather hadn't been out of town while Nick was engaged with his father's death and the aftermath, another of the Phoenix Brotherhood would have moved in.

"Any luck getting any new information from the DOA?" Nick asked.

"We've found nothing out of the ordinary in the personnel files of the three names you've identified. And no luck identifying any of the others. The battalion commander and the lieutenant in charge of your father's platoon were both killed in combat. We've managed to track down a couple of people who were there at the same time as your dad, but we've gotten no hits on the nicknames. And no knowledge of anything the three men you've identified might have been involved in together. No suggestion of drug dealing.

No criminal activity of any kind. Not that they remember."

"Cara and I met with an executive assistant director at the FBI this morning. Someone named Ainsworth. He admits that the Bureau is having second thoughts about Crawford's heart attack, but as far as he's aware, there was no connection to Vietnam in anything Crawford was working on."

"You believe him?"

"I don't know. I didn't like him, but then bureaucracy generally makes my flesh crawl. He sounded as if he was spouting the party line in hopes that we'd give him something."

"Did you?"

"We didn't have a choice. Not if we wanted some reciprocal cooperation. And I couldn't see where it could hurt. If someone at the Bureau is behind this, then they have been ahead of us the whole way. I told him what we've managed to piece together. He didn't seem impressed with my theory and he didn't promise to look into Crawford's files."

"How long between the time you left his office and the ambush?"

"Not long enough," Nick acknowledged. "Why? You know him?"

"I've heard the name, but that isn't really why I asked. I'm just wondering how someone was able to breach security at the estate. That's a pretty sophisticated setup."

Knowing Griff, who came from the same wealthy background as his wife's family, the Gardner property would have the best security money could buy.

"As you and I both know," Nick reminded him, "there's nothing that can't be gotten around."

The External Security Team had had their own experts who could seemingly walk through walls. All it took was cutting-edge technology and some prior knowledge of the system you were dealing with.

Which was why Griff had posed his original question. The FBI would be one of the entities in this town that would have both the technology and the expertise. The CIA would be the other.

"I'll send a team out to the estate to see what they can discover," Cabot said. "What can I do for you in the meantime?"

"Check out Ainsworth. And keep working on those names. There's got to be someone left from that company who knows how these six men are connected to something that's getting them murdered."

"We're making the calls," Griff promised.

It would be a slow process, tracking down men whose addresses of record would be at least a quarter of a century out of date. And with Nick on leave, the agency was already operating with reduced manpower.

"Look, I know this isn't really the Phoenix's concern—" Nick began, only to be cut off.

"It is now. It was as soon as you asked for our help. The name may have changed, but the concept hasn't."

From the External Security Team to the Phoenix Brotherhood. Though they'd had losses through the years, protecting one another, as well as the country they served, had always been a priority.

"Do you need somewhere to stay?" Cabot went on without giving Nick time to respond to his reminder. "The beach house is still secure."

"We checked into the Wardman. Ainsworth is supposed to let us know what he finds out. I'd like to stay in town at least until I hear from him. Oh, and I ditched my car because I thought they might have attached a transmitter while it was parked at the airport. If someone could pick it up and make sure it's clean…"

Nick gave Griff the address where he'd left the Jeep and then agreed to his superior's demand to stay in touch. He felt as if he should say something about how much he appreciated the agency's help and support, but he wasn't good at that kind of thing. Besides, Cabot had already made it clear he didn't want to hear any expressions of gratitude.

Nick hung up, his throat a little tight from that unexpressed emotion. He raised his eyes to find Cara watching him again.

"They're going to pick up the car and make sure it's clean," he said unnecessarily.

She nodded, her hand still making that now-automatic journey up and down the opposite arm.

"I'm sorry," he said.

Whatever she'd been expecting, it obviously wasn't an apology. "What for?"

"For letting you walk into the middle of an ambush."

She nodded again, her eyes still on his face. He knew he needed to tell her the rest of it, but he wasn't good at this, either. Still…

"And for yelling at you."

"I thought you meant for me to come to the Jeep. I'd been watching the sniper, and when I turned around… I don't know. I thought you'd been gesturing for me to make that move."

Nick shook his head, trying to remember anything he'd done that might have given her that impression. There was no reason for her to leave what was—relatively speaking—a safe location.

"I was probably checking to make sure you were all right. Whatever happened doesn't matter now. I just wanted to say that I know I had no right to yell at you."

He wasn't yet ready to confess that seeing her running across that open expanse had turned his guts to water. There would come a time when he'd have the freedom to tell her how he felt. At least he hoped there would. But until he got a handle on the bastards who were after them as well as the men in his father's unit, his personal feelings should remain exactly that. Personal.

"I thought it was about time I pulled my share of the load."

"Your share of the load?" he repeated, that same cold, unpleasant stirring in his gut. "What does that mean?"

"I thought maybe if I could draw his fire—"

For a second the words made no sense, and when they did, he strode across the room to grab her shoulders, just as he had at the guesthouse. "You were *trying* to get him to shoot at you. Is that what you're telling me?"

His fury was almost as great as that which had been fueled by his fear. When he realized how angry he was, he forced his hands to release her, stepping back before he lost control.

"I know it was stupid—"

"You've got that right. When I want you to make a target of yourself—" He stopped because the very thought was exactly what she'd said. Stupid.

"I'm trying to protect you," he went on, the words carefully enunciated. "I'm certainly not going to ask you to take that kind of risk. How the hell you ever came up with something like that—"

He ground to a stop, the look in her eyes telling him that he'd said enough. What had happened this afternoon wouldn't happen again.

"Because I'm not," she said softly. "I haven't been from the first."

Pulling her share of the load. She was back to that. He couldn't imagine what she thought he expected from her.

And then he remembered. He had involved her in this because of her expertise in an area where he had believed she might prove helpful.

"I know you don't understand why I refused to breach the system, but…if there *was* something in those files, it probably isn't there any longer. With Crawford's death, they may have—"

"That doesn't matter. Just don't ever pull a stunt like that again. I'm never going to deliberately put you into danger. So don't react to what you *think* I might want you to do. When I need you to make a move, there'll be no doubt about what it is. And for God's sake, no matter what happens, don't you ever assume I'm willingly putting you in harm's way."

He had already done that, simply by bringing her with him, but it was too late to turn back the clock on that decision. She was his responsibility. His to keep safe until this was over.

Her eyes, still raised to his, indicated how defeated she felt. The only thing he wanted to do right now was to take her into his arms and promise her that he wouldn't let anything bad ever happen to her.

It was too late to maintain the emotional distance he needed to carry out this mission. If something happened to Cara, he wouldn't be able to accept it as he had the so-called "collateral damage" he'd dealt with in the military or on the External Security Team.

If anything happened to Cara, it would be his fault. And for him that would be far worse than accepting his own death.

Chapter Sixteen

The first knock had been expected. Room service had delivered their dinner less than an hour ago. Although she had never in her life felt less like eating, Cara had forced down the sandwich and chips. She had also drunk a cup of the coffee Nick ordered. The caffeine had given her enough of a boost that she no longer felt like the world's greatest failure.

The second knock, about an hour later, had obviously been unexpected, causing Nick to draw his gun on the way to answer the door.

"Who is it?" he asked peering out through the peephole.

"Dalton Rawls."

The name meant nothing to Cara, but the identification, combined with whatever he'd seen outside, caused Nick to immediately throw the latch and disengage the chain. When the door opened, Cara could see the man in the hallway. He was holding a suitcase in each hand, one of them her weekender and the other Nick's bag.

"Griff thought you might need these," Rawls said.

"Come in," Nick instructed, looking up and down the hallway as soon as his visitor had followed his instructions. He closed and relocked the door before he turned to make the introduction.

"Cara, this is Dalton Rawls, a member of the Phoenix. Dalton, Cara Simonson."

"Ms. Simonson," Rawls said, inclining his head.

He was above average height, maybe six-one or six-two. Despite the well-cut suit he wore, it was apparent he was less heavily muscled than Nick. His frame was leaner, although his shoulders were as broad.

His hair was a dark chestnut touched with lighter streaks, obviously burned there by the sun that had darkened his skin. His eyes, a clear, unusual shade of green, had seemed almost amused when he'd greeted her.

Because he'd been ordered to bring their luggage to them? Or because something about her expression had revealed her discomfort over that situation?

Which was patently ridiculous, she told herself. No one gave a damn about her being in a hotel room with Nick. The fact that she had even considered what this man might be thinking was almost as ridiculous as believing she could do something to help this afternoon.

"Mr. Rawls," she said.

Not only had she stammered slightly over his name, but she could feel heat staining her cheeks. She held her chin high, refusing to make any other display of her embarrassment.

Of course, Nick's fellow agent was handsome enough that he was probably accustomed to women being disconcerted by that direct gaze. His good looks were classic, although personally she was more attracted to Nick's rugged features.

And to everything else about him.

"This is yours, I believe," Rawls said, holding out her suitcase. Given the choice between Nick's battered black canvas bag and her designer case, it wasn't surprising he'd known which was which.

"Thanks," she said, walking over to take it.

"And Griff thought you might like these," Rawls said.

Surprised, Cara looked up only to realize that he was holding out an envelope to Nick. He had already taken his own bag, which he dropped onto the foot of the bed in order to take whatever else Cabot had sent him.

"Those are the complete personnel records of the three men you've identified. They include dates of service and any other information available about their years in the military. There are also a couple of possibilities in there for the John on your father's list, both in his platoon. One of those died in Vietnam a couple of months after your father came home. The other committed suicide twelve years ago. We're still running down the other Johns in the battalion around the pertinent time period, but as you can imagine, it's a time-consuming process."

"I know," Nick said almost absently.

"We've also interviewed a couple of people we were able to locate who were in the platoon during that time frame. Neither of them remembered anything that might be helpful."

It seemed to Cara that Nick's friends had accomplished a lot in a very limited amount of time. Just nothing, sadly, that made a substantial difference.

"Griff said to let him know if you think of anything else that we might be doing…"

The Phoenix operative let the sentence trail, watching Nick thumb through the documents he'd provided. At some point Dalton Rawls became aware that she was watching him, maybe to better understand the man she was so attracted to by learning something about his associates. He turned to smile at her.

Compared to Nick, he seemed almost ordinary. Safe. Certainly not like the experienced covert operative he probably was.

"Thanks," Nick said, finally glancing up from the papers he'd been given. "Would you tell Griff how much—" He broke the sentence, obviously searching for the right words.

"He knows," Rawls said. "We've all been here before. Even Griff."

Nick nodded without attempting to express his gratitude again. There was a heartbeat of silence before he asked instead, "I don't suppose they found the intruder on the estate?"

"We found evidence of where he set up his ambush. We still don't know exactly how he overrode the security system, but apparently it was done electronically. Griff's been in contact with the company, who'll have their people out to check on the breakdown tomorrow."

"I'd appreciate a call about what they find."

"Consider it done. Oh, and by the way, your car's in the hotel's underground garage. There was no transmitter."

"Thanks."

"If you think of anything else, you know where to reach us," Rawls offered again. "Ms. Simonson." He nodded to her, his smile broader this time and more relaxed.

"It was very nice to have met you," she said, thinking as the words came out of her mouth how inane they were. Considering why he was here.

"Maybe the next time we'll meet in less...unusual circumstances."

The comment sounded as if he expected to see her again. Maybe even wanted to. Why in the world would a man like this want another meeting with her? Unless...

Unusual circumstances? For a second, the sense of embarrassment she'd felt when Dalton had entered the room she and Nick were sharing returned before she realized he had referenced to what had happened at the estate today.

"I hope so," she said, returning his smile.

She glanced at Nick, surprising something that looked like the same cold anger she'd seen in his eyes this afternoon. She couldn't imagine what she'd said that might have caused it.

Her conversation with Dalton Rawls had certainly been mundane enough. Neither of them had mentioned anything to do with the investigation.

The Phoenix operative held out his hand to Nick, seemingly oblivious to the undercurrent she was aware of. Nick's mouth had tightened, but he shook the outstretched hand before he escorted his guest to the door, leaving Cara to figure out what had happened to put him in a foul mood.

When he had closed the door behind Rawls, Nick turned back, studying her a moment before he said, "I think it might be better if you go to your aunt's."

"What?" That suggestion was the last thing she expected. Again, she was at a loss for what had produced this about-face. "Why would I do that now?"

"Because this isn't working," Nick said.

She bit back the retort that sprang to mind. She knew he was frustrated, but it wasn't her fault they weren't any closer to the next name on the list.

Or maybe he thought it was her fault. Maybe that's why he was angry. If she had done what he had wanted her to do at the beginning and tried to get access to Crawford's files, maybe he believed things might be different now. Maybe McGregor wouldn't be dead.

She was under no illusion about why Nick had brought her this far. He'd been hoping that through her access to the Bureau's database, she could help him find his father's killers. And she had consistently refused to cooperate.

Added to that was what she'd done this afternoon. She was no longer an asset, but a liability.

She understood that. She could even sympathize with it. The problem was that her stake in this was as great as Nick's. After all, they had murdered her father, too. She wasn't ready to give up her own quest for justice. And for answers.

"Look," she began, trying for a rationality she didn't feel. "I know that what I did this afternoon was stupid. I've already apologized for it. I misunderstood what you wanted me to do."

"It isn't that."

"Then what is it?"

The dark eyes were still focused on her face. For several seconds he didn't say anything. And when he did, it wasn't any more revealing than what he'd told her before.

"This is just not a good idea."

"I know you think I'm just a complication. Someone you have to look out for. But I promise you nothing like that will happen again. When we started all this, I didn't know what to expect. I had no idea how ruthless these people were. I'm not that naive anymore."

"There are too many things that could go wrong."

"Like a hit-and-run? Or an explosion?" It seemed a little late in the day to be worried about putting her in harm's way. "What's changed all of a sudden?"

"I had thought your connection to the Bureau might speed things along, and maybe it has, although not in the way I'd envisioned. For what it's worth, I think Ainsworth will talk to me now, even if you're not along. So...there's no longer any reason for you to be involved."

No longer any reason for you to be involved. She wasn't sure why the words hurt as much as they did, but she didn't deny their pain. It was becoming clear Nick really did want her to leave.

"There's still one very good reason," she reminded him almost bitterly. "My father's dead, too. That gives me the *right* to be here. A right to be *involved.*"

He had the grace not to answer the overt sarcasm in her repetition of his word. He simply stood before the door to the hallway, his face hard.

"Are you afraid I'll get in the way again?" she prodded, still trying to understand what had brought this on right now. "Did I do or say something wrong in front of your friend? What's happened that makes you so determined to get me out of here?"

He owed her an answer. She hadn't asked to come along on this ride. Nick had come to her. He had enlisted her help in this one-man war he'd been waging.

Even as the thought formed, she knew that was part of it. This *was* a one-man war. That was the only way Nick Morelli knew how to fight. Him against the world. And when there was someone else involved, someone who cared about what happened to him—

That was it, she realized suddenly. Inadvertently, she had somehow revealed how she felt about him. That's what this was all about. Her growing feelings for this difficult loner. Feelings he wanted no part of.

She reached that conclusion simultaneously with Nick's first step away from the door. He literally stalked across the room, determination revealed in every taut muscle of his body.

As he came closer, she realized that she was almost afraid of him in this mood. Very much aware, just as she had been on the day of her father's funeral, of the explosiveness of his temperament.

She refused to let him see her fear, holding her ground as he approached. Nick stopped in front of her, looking down into her face for a long moment. He wasn't that much taller than she, so that her chin was tilted upward at a perfect angle when his lips began their descent to hers.

Given the bitterness each of them had just expressed, the kiss was unexpected. That didn't keep her from responding. As soon as his mouth made contact, her lips parted, her tongue straining to meet his. To match it movement for movement.

It seemed as if she had been waiting for this forever. Since the day he'd taken her arm to draw her onto the sunporch at her mother's house. Since his almost boastful promise the first night they'd spent together. Certainly since the interrupted kiss outside that motel in Tennessee.

Cheap motel. The words—and all they stood for— echoed in her head as his lips continued to ravage hers.

There was nothing gentle about the kiss. It was as hard and demanding as the man who held her, the corded muscles in his arms and chest powerful enough to break her in two, just as his kiss had broken any will she might have had to resist.

He began to unbutton her blouse, his fingers hurrying over the task. The callused skin of his palm caught against the silk as they moved relentlessly down the placket.

She knew she should tell him to stop. She should just put her fingers over his and push them away before this got completely out of hand. He had just been trying to send her away, and now—

His hand slipped inside the opening he'd created. The unexpected, totally masculine feel of it moving against the skin of her stomach took her breath. And with it, any thoughts of refusal.

The hooks of her bra were unfastened with an expertise that told her guns and explosions weren't the only things with which Nick Morelli had experience. Once the clasp was loosened, he didn't bother any further with the garment. He simply pushed it out of his way as his mouth lowered toward her exposed breast.

Her eyes closed in anticipation, but nothing could have prepared her for the sensation of his lips closing around her nipple. Where his kiss had been demanding, almost controlling, the movement of his mouth over her suddenly tautening flesh was the merest touch. A brush of lips. A slow circling of hot, wet tongue.

She was vulnerable in a way she had never allowed herself to be before. Her brains and her innate shyness had kept most men at bay through the years. The few who had not been discouraged by that combination had been nothing like Nick Morelli.

Like the one-man war he was waging against his father's murderers, this, too, was outside her area of expertise. Almost outside the boundaries of her very limited experience.

His lips closed over the hardened nub he had created, instantly destroying all logical thought process. He suckled, the pressure strong enough to evoke a matching ache deep within her body.

Her fingers locked spasmodically in his hair. She was unsure whether the gesture was intended as a protest or an attempt to hold him to her.

Obviously it didn't matter. As he had ravaged her mouth with his kiss, he continued to caress her oversensitized breast.

Her skin was being slightly chafed by his late-day whiskers. And like the sensation of his callused palm moving over the smooth skin of her stomach, she found the abrasion incredibly sensuous.

Then, in addition to his lips, he began to employ his teeth, teasing her nipple until the feeling he created balanced on the delicate edge between pleasure and pain. She didn't want him to stop, however, even if it slipped over to the latter.

Actually, her greatest fear was that he might remember that he'd been trying to get her to leave.

His mouth deserted her breast, leaving it damp and aching for his touch. The exposure to the cool air of the room was different—not nearly so satisfying an experience as the caress of his lips. She opened her eyes to discover what had happened.

Nick was in the process of jerking the tail of his shirt out of his jeans. Then, when it was only partially free, he reached behind his neck and, grabbing a hand-ful of fabric, pulled both shirt and undershirt off over his head.

He dropped the garments on the floor, immediately stepping forward to put his arms around her. Despite the awkwardness of her disarrayed garments, some-how he managed to pull her against him so that her clothing didn't impede the flesh-to-flesh contact he sought.

Her nipples, already sensitized, brushed against a hair-roughened wall of muscle as his lips closed over hers once more. Her knees went weak, so that she was forced to put her arms around his neck simply to stay upright.

As she did, her body moved into perfect alignment with his, so that she could feel not only the rapid-fire beating of his heart, but also the strength of his erec-tion.

For a second—less than a heartbeat—she was again afraid. Frightened this time of the unleashed power of Nick Morelli. It was something that, on some level, she had always been aware of. But not in this context. Not sexually.

Just as her ultimatum had been, this was the mo-ment of truth. In another few seconds it would be too late to back out. Too late to remind him of all the rea-sons this shouldn't be happening.

Right now, she couldn't think of a single one of them. All she could think of was the hardness of his chest moving against the softness of her breasts.

She shifted her hands, so that her palms were against the jut of collarbone on each shoulder. In re-sponse to the pressure they exerted, he lifted his lips from hers, just enough that she could hear the harshness of his breathing. It was the only sound in the dimness of the hotel room.

She tried to think what she needed to say, but it was impossible to arrange her doubts into a coherent argument with his hips pressed so intimately against hers. Reminding her that she had let this go on too far before she had thought about stopping it. But if she didn't now…

"I don't think we should—"

With the first tremulous breath she'd drawn in order to voice her protest, she felt his body stiffen.

"Shut up," he whispered, interrupting that tentative protest. "Just shut the hell up, Cara, and kiss me."

His breath felt warm and moist against her cheek. Exactly as his lips had when they'd nuzzled her nipple. Just before they had closed over it to drive her to the brink of insanity.

This was the same kind of moment. If she gave in to that seductive whisper and did what he wanted, there would be no turning back.

"Nick…"

"Are you telling me no?" The question was abrupt, its tone as harsh as when he'd yelled at her at the estate.

What the hell did you think you were doing?

It was probably a better question now than it had been then. She hadn't had a clue what she was supposed to do in a situation like the one they'd faced at the estate today, but she had no doubt what she should be doing now.

Are you telling me no?

If she did, she knew enough about Nick's self-discipline by now to understand that no matter how far this had gone, he would again take that step back. Releasing her. Allowing the cold, lonely air to caress her skin instead of his lips.

He had already made the decision to send her away. If she told him no, this might be the last time he ever touched her.

And it would be *her* decision. She had known that even when he had promised the first night that he would make love to her.

When I make love to you...

Not *if*, but *when*. He had known even then that this was inevitable. Maybe she had, too.

"Cara?"

Her decision. One that she, too, had probably made that first night.

"No, Nick," she whispered, "I'm not telling you no."

Chapter Seventeen

Nick had reached over and flicked off the bedside lamp before he'd undressed her, knowing instinctively that she would be far more comfortable with the lights off. Maybe she wasn't telling him no, but he understood that she wasn't sure this was something she was ready for.

That was all right with him. He had all night to convince her.

He intended to use every minute of it for that purpose. He had no objections to slow and deliberate.

The self-control he prided himself on spiraled away into the darkness, however, as soon as he'd laid Cara on the bed. There was just enough light in the room to allow his eyes to trace over each curve and secret hollow. Her skin was alabaster in the dimness, distinguishable from the whiteness of the sheets only by the living, breathing contours of her body.

It possessed the same classic beauty he had noticed in her features the first time he'd seen her. A slender neck set above delicate shoulders. Breasts the perfect size for a man's hand to cup and his mouth to kiss. A narrow waist that that flared to hips that were perhaps wider than the current fashion, but perfect for the two things a woman's hips were designed for: lovemaking and childbearing.

Childbearing...

Nick couldn't remember ever before thinking about a woman carrying his child. Without his conscious volition, his eyes touched on Cara's flat belly before he jerked his gaze away.

He was in way over his head. He had known that since his overreaction to Cara being in danger this afternoon. And he had had that knowledge reinforced tonight when he'd sensed Dalton's attraction.

He had no right to feel the way he had about that. He had no claim on Cara Simonson. He had been careful to make no promises.

When I make love to you...

No promises except that, he amended. Which he was about to keep.

He put his knee on the mattress beside her and realized she was watching him, her eyes wide and dark. Maybe she was looking for reassurance. Waiting for him to say something about what was about to happen between them. Waiting for him to tell her how he felt.

He hoped to hell that wasn't what she was expecting. He'd never been good at talking about what he was feeling. If he couldn't show her—

Her hand lifted—long, slim fingers reaching upward to touch his face. The unexpected gesture froze him in place.

With her forefinger she traced along his bottom lip. Her hand continued until it lay along the side of his face.

"It's all right," she said softly. "Everything's all right."

Her reassurance broke the spell that had held him.

As his body lowered over hers in the darkness, he swore that before the night was over she would have no doubt about his feelings. He just didn't intend to use words to communicate them.

SHE'D LOST COUNT of the number of times Nick had brought her to climax. All she knew was that each had been more powerful and uncontrollable than the last. And each had been the result of an inexhaustible patience, an unquestioned expertise, and a desire— seemingly—to do nothing but please her.

He had made love to her in ways she hadn't known existed. Ways that, if she thought about them, might have embarrassed her. He hadn't given her time to think, and he had wisely ignored her first tentative attempts to object—until she no longer had any reason to want to.

There were no secrets between them now. He knew her body intimately. He had explored it with his hands and lips and tongue. He had examined every muscle and bone, leaving them weak and sated in the wake of his lovemaking.

Lovemaking.

That was exactly what he had done. Nick had made love to her, although he had never whispered that word—or any others—while he was doing it. He had simply concentrated on given her pleasure in a hundred different ways.

And now again she lay spent as the waves of sensation retreated, leaving her once more mindless with pleasure. Boneless with satisfaction.

She opened her eyes to find him propped on one elbow, looking down on her in the darkness. Her lips tilted automatically, but he didn't return the smile. His rugged features seemed carved in stone. Implacable.

"What's wrong?"

He shook his head, bending to drop a kiss on her still-open lips. She smiled at him again as his head lifted.

The moonlight filtering into the room through the sheers over the windows cast half his face in shadow, giving him an almost sinister look. It would be hard for her to remember anything other than the side of him he'd shown her tonight, despite what she knew about his past.

"Am I supposed to cry 'uncle' or something?" she asked, raising her hand to touch his hair.

"What does that mean?"

"That I surrender. Give up. Need to come up for air."

"Do you?"

"All of the above. Except..."

"Except what?"

With one finger he had begun to trace a path from the center of her chest down to her navel. As she attempted to frame an answer to his question, it tracked lower. Unbelievably, despite the fact that she was beyond satiation, a quiver of anticipation flickered through her body.

"This all seems...a little one-sided."

She took a deep breath to control the sensations he was creating. His thumb continued to brush lightly back and forth across her lower stomach while his middle finger explored territory with which he was already very familiar.

"Maybe."

"That hardly seems fair."

"So what did you have in mind?"

Almost nothing, she thought in response to a suddenly far more intimate exploration. If he continued, soon there would be nothing at all left in her mind.

"Something for you?" she suggested when she was able to speak again.

"How very unselfish."

"Not really. I have a pretty good idea I'd enjoy the experience, too."

He nodded, lips pursed as if he were giving her proposal serious consideration. All the while his fingers continued to move. If he didn't decide pretty soon…

"I guess there's only one way to find out."

He moved, his body suddenly looming above hers in the darkness. And then, as he held her eyes, he lowered his hips, sliding into the ready warmth and wetness he had created.

Waiting for him. Waiting for this.

Everything that had come before had been prelude. Prologue. Overture.

This was the drama. The reality.

What he had made her feel had been incredible, but it had been hers alone. This was theirs. Something that would forever belong exclusively to them.

Whether it was the emotional impact of that realization or whether all the other times he had brought her to this place had made the pathway too familiar, she was suddenly there. At the peak. Waiting for the conflagration that was the inevitable result of applying spark to this particular tinder.

She closed her eyes, making an attempt to control what was about to happen. Another powerful downward stroke, and she knew it was far too late. The tremors began deep inside her body, growing in intensity until she was forced to give in to their demand.

She surrendered to the tide of sensation—the last conscious thought she was capable of was the realization that he had joined her. His body moved above hers, the rhythm he had begun shattering in its own cataclysm. She opened her eyes, determined to watch as he experienced the same satisfaction he had given her so many times tonight.

His neck arched, tendons taut and straining. He made no sound, but his mouth opened, his breathing harsh.

As ecstasy shivered into stillness inside her body, his was racked with the ultimate paroxysm. Still she watched his face, unable to look away.

When it was over, he collapsed against her, resting his entire weight on top of her for a long heartbeat. Almost immediately he shifted, lifting his torso by propping on his elbows.

A dozen sensations assaulted her simultaneously. The heat of his body. The hardness of it. The fact that they were still intimately joined, despite the passing of the storm. His slowly softening erection. The moisture that created a seal along the entire length of their bodies, binding them together. The sound of their breathing.

For a long time neither of them said anything. Waiting, perhaps, to regain the breath and sanity necessary to form words.

And when she had, the ones that were in her head—and in her heart—were the very ones she had promised herself she would not say.

"Please don't send me away."

Her whisper faded into a stillness not even their breathing disturbed.

"It isn't safe. I can't keep you safe."

"It doesn't matter." It was a foolish thing to say, but at this moment it didn't. Not to her.

"It does to me."

"That isn't your job. Keeping me safe. I never was your responsibility. And if you somehow feel I am, I absolve you of it."

There was another silence, but she waited through it, knowing that despite everything she could say or do, this decision wouldn't be up to her. All she could do was hope that what had happened between them tonight would lead him to make the right one.

"If anything happened to you…"

She waited, but he didn't finish the thought.

"Nick?"

"I couldn't *absolve* myself," he said. "I'm not sure I could live with that."

The words repeated over and over in her head as she tried to make them mean anything other than what they *must* mean. When she couldn't, her heart rate accelerated so that she knew he would be able to feel it beating under his.

"Why?"

She was asking for heartbreak. He wouldn't answer that. Not even if he had really meant what those words implied. He would *never* say it aloud.

"When this is over…"

The words faded. Again she waited through the silence. After a moment, his body lifted away from hers.

She closed her eyes, aware of what was happening by the shift of his weight off the mattress. She didn't open them, not even when she knew she was alone in the bed.

When this is over…

He had made another promise when whatever this was between them had just begun. *When I make love to you…*

That one he had kept. All she could do now was wait—and hope—that he would keep this one, as well.

Chapter Eighteen

When Cara awoke, dawn was creeping in through the sheers over the windows. She didn't move, savoring the feel of Nick's body against hers. And remembering all that had happened between them last night.

A week ago she hadn't even known this man. Now she did—intimately. As he knew her.

She felt a touch of anxiety about the speed with which they'd reached this point. Like everything else about the last few days, that, too, was outside the realm of her experience. Her previous relationships had been slowly developed, building on friendship, common interests and trust, before they had moved on to anything sexual. This...

This had been like a fast-moving storm. Almost before you had time to be aware of the wind and the first few drops of rain, it had swept over you with gale force—complete with lightning and thunder.

She hadn't intended to end up in bed with Nick last night. And she certainly hadn't intended to feel about him the way she did this morning.

She turned, propping on one elbow, so she could see him, being careful not to wake him. His face, relaxed now in sleep, made him appear vulnerable, even more so than during the first couple of days when he'd been injured.

The whiskers that had been a faint five-o'clock shadow last night were as black as his hair. Thick lashes rested over the fragile skin beneath his eyes, slightly discolored from a lack of sleep. She was responsible for that. At least for last night's loss.

She allowed her eyes to continue their examination, moving across the broad, darkly tanned chest to the flat stomach, bisected by that dark arrow of hair. It was a sight that had taken her breath the first time she'd seen it. It still did. The sheet covered his body from the hips down, which was just as well for her peace of mind.

She thought briefly about easing back down against his side and trying to go back to sleep, but she needed to go to the bathroom. And, more pressing than that, she needed time to think. Time to adjust to the fundamental change that had occurred in their relationship. Neither of those could be as easily accomplished in Nick's arms.

She eased out of bed and then stood beside it for a long moment, watching him sleep. The regular rise and fall of his breathing hadn't changed despite her movements. Of course, with the pain he'd been in from his ribs, he'd missed far more sleep than she had during the past few nights.

She resisted the urge to bend and kiss the parted lips. She knew what would happen if she awakened him. And right now—

Right now, she reiterated, she needed time to think. And she needed to do that away from the temptation Nick represented.

Before she went into the bathroom to shower and

dress, she pulled the lined drapes over the sheers at the windows, effectively blocking the pale sunlight that was just beginning to brighten the room. As she headed again toward the bath, she noticed the envelope Dalton Rawls had handed Nick last night.

Other than the cursory thumb-through he'd afforded it as soon as he'd had it in his hands, Nick hadn't had a chance to study it. They'd been occupied with other things after the Phoenix agent left.

There was probably nothing in those papers they didn't already know. Still…

On impulse she picked the envelope up off the dresser and carried it into the bathroom with her. There she could turn on the light and look at what it contained without the chance of waking Nick.

AS SOON AS HE OPENED his eyes, he knew by the quality of the light seeping around the edges of the drapes that it was late. It took him a second or two longer to come to the realization that he was alone in the bed where he had slept through the night holding Cara.

Cara.

Where the hell was she? He sat up so quickly that for a moment he was literally light-headed.

The wave of panic subsided when his searching eyes found her seated at the desk the hotel had thoughtfully provided. In the dimness of the room, the screen of her laptop cast a glow over her features.

She was so intent on whatever she was doing that she wasn't yet aware he was awake. He glanced over at the bedside clock. The digital display informed him that it was almost eleven. Long past the time when he should be up, he acknowledged guiltily.

Despite the fact that they seemed to have gone as

far as they could with this without getting some kind of break, he owed it to the men on his father's list to keep trying. Just as he owed it to his father.

He sat up on the edge of the bed, immediately reminded of the damage his ribs had sustained. Something he hadn't been aware of very much yesterday. Well worth the price, he decided, stretching the muscles in his back and shoulders by turning his head from side to side. He glanced at Cara again, but her focus was still totally on the computer.

He stood up, pulling the disordered top sheet off the bed. He wrapped it around his waist as he walked toward the desk.

From looking at the screen of the laptop, it was obvious that Cara was sending an e-mail. To her mother? Somehow Miriam didn't seem the type for that form of communication. Or maybe Cara's message was intended for her boss. After all, she had probably missed more days of work than she'd initially planned.

He watched the cursor hit the send button. Then, as he bent to kiss her just below the ear, he asked, "What are you doing?"

Cara jumped, apparently startled to find him behind her. She turned, her face immediately relaxing into a smile. She was wearing her nightshirt, although she smelled of soap and shampoo and toothpaste, making it obvious she'd already showered. And making him aware that he hadn't.

"Did you know that my dad and yours were only in 'Nam at the same time for little more than a week?"

He straightened, the delectable curve of her jaw forgotten as he tried to process what she'd just said. "Are you sure?"

"Unless the records your friend brought over last night are wrong. Look at the dates."

She pushed the papers that were spread out beside her toward him. One was his dad's service record; the other was her father's.

And she was right, Nick realized. There was a period of only ten days between Simonson's arrival in country and his father's departure. He had never really known when his dad returned to the States. He'd been too young to remember that homecoming.

Although he could probably have come close to Simonson's dates of service from the postmarks on his letters, he hadn't bothered. The exact date hadn't seemed that important. All that had mattered at that point was that they had been there at the same time. If the dates he was looking at were accurate, however, they substantially narrowed the time frame of whatever had happened.

"And that's the date my dad arrived in country," Cara went on, "*not* at battalion."

Which meant, that with processing, orientation, transportation and whatever else the army deemed essential, Simonson might not have reported to his unit until his own father had already left.

"And he wasn't even assigned to the same platoon," Cara went on. The excitement in her eyes over what she'd discovered was clearly revealed by the light from the screen. "McGregor was. They had served together almost seven months when your dad's tour was up. So whatever happened—"

"According to the people Griff has interviewed who were in the platoon at that time, *nothing* happened."

"Then maybe it happened while they weren't with the platoon. While they were in transport."

"Except they would have had to be traveling in opposite directions. Your dad coming in. My dad going out. And McGregor didn't leave—" He glanced down at the pile on the desk, pushing pages aside until he located the right one. "Until five months later."

"Okay," she said, sitting down on the other end of the couch. "Morelli's leaving country and Simonson is arriving. How are they doing that?"

"You mean…?"

"How are they being transported?"

"By helicopter," he said grudgingly. There was a dull ache behind his eyes. He needed coffee. Maybe if he could see where this was going… "Helicopters flying in opposite directions," he reiterated.

"Like ships that pass in the night," Cara said. There was a note in her voice that he couldn't quite identify. It had sounded almost…triumphant. "That's exactly what I thought when I looked at those dates. My father was coming in. And within a few days, yours was going out. So…I did a search."

"What kind of search?" Despite her eagerness to explain what she thought she'd found—or maybe because of it—he wasn't following.

"Look."

She touched the thumb pad on the keyboard, and the text of the e-mail disappeared to be replaced with a Web page containing a picture of a helicopter, its nose painted red with white teeth like those old World War II planes Chenault's Flying Tigers had flown. Young men in uniform, looking eerily similar to the ones in the photographs he'd found beside his father's chair, smiled at the camera.

"I don't understand."

"The 174th Assault Helicopter Company. They also

operated out of Duc Pho. Apparently it was a fairly big base with both infantry and air support."

Unconsciously he shook his head, failing to make the connection she had obviously seen. Maybe they had been on the same base—

"They're the Sharks, Nick," she said softly, pausing to give him time to assimilate her revelation before she added, "That was the nickname of the company."

The Sharks. Was the notation on his father's list not the nickname of a person, as he'd assumed, but of a helicopter unit? The Shark. Or one of its pilots, someone who had witnessed whatever had gotten his father murdered.

Could those six men on the list, by some fluke of wartime transportation, have all ended up on the same chopper? Except—

"Those are gunships. Not transports," he said flatly. "They wouldn't have been used for carrying troops."

"*Never?* You can't know that. All kinds of things happen in war. Maybe the transport helicopters they were on were shot down or had engine trouble and these guys were called in for rescue. This *has* to mean something, Nick. The Shark. That's the only one of those nicknames she included a modifier for. This *has* to be what your dad was talking about. You're the one who told me that you eventually reach a point where things can't be put down to coincidence."

Maybe she was right. He couldn't imagine how the pilot of one of those gunships might play into the scenario of arrival and departure the service records described, but 'Nam *had* been a war where things didn't always happen according to the rules.

"Even if you're right…I'm not sure how much this helps."

Rather than narrowing their search from battalion level to platoon or even squad, as he'd hoped to do from the service records, this expanded it. If "The Shark" on his father's list had reference to a pilot, then possibilities had been opened up beyond the parameters they'd been working from before.

"I sent them an e-mail," Cara said. "I know it's a long shot, but now that we have a specific time period—"

"You sent *who* an e-mail?" he demanded, again not following the progression.

"The 174th. They have a Listserv, an e-mail loop that allows the veterans of the unit to stay in touch. I asked the Web master to pass my message on to the people who are on that list. I said that we were trying to track down something that happened during that particular week. Something serious enough that someone would be willing to kill to keep it a secret."

"And you think someone's going to *respond* to that?"

"I think we won't know unless we try," she said stiffly. "Maybe no one will know what I'm talking about. Maybe they won't respond, but...maybe whatever happened has bothered one of them all these years, just as it apparently did my dad."

An event that had pushed her father along the path to alcoholism? And had embittered his own father to the point of estrangement with all the people who had once cared about him?

"Nick? I'm sorry if—"

Whatever apology she was about to make was interrupted by the ringing of his cell phone. He turned, crossing the room to grab it off the bedside table on the third ring.

"Morelli."

"Richard Ainsworth, Mr. Morelli. I've done some preliminary investigation on what we talked about. And I've located someone I think you ought to talk to. I wondered if you and Ms. Simonson might be available for a meeting this afternoon, say two o'clock?"

If Ainsworth had bothered to check out anything they'd told him, Nick had believed the Bureau would want to pursue the connection between their agent's death and those of the men on his father's list. He was surprised, however, at the speed with which the assistant executive director had gotten back to them.

Maybe Ainsworth had turned up something in Crawford's files. And at this point, when their own investigation had come down to an e-mail sent to a veterans' group's Listserv, Nick figured he had nothing to lose by listening to whatever the Bureau had to tell him.

"We'll be there," he said.

"Good. I'm looking forward to it."

Chapter Nineteen

Ainsworth's secretary seemed welcoming as she ushered them into his office. This time there were three chairs lined up in front of his desk, one of them occupied by a white-haired man who appeared to be in his sixties. He stood as they entered, his posture immediately indicating a military background to Nick.

"Ms. Simonson. Mr. Morelli. I'd like you to meet Lieutenant Colonel Ron Kittering, U.S. Army retired. He was the commander of the company your fathers served in. I thought he might be able to shed some light on the questions you had."

The colonel inclined his head to Cara and then held out his hand to Nick. Despite his age, Kittering's handclasp, unlike Ainsworth's yesterday, was firm, his palm slightly callused. Piercing blue eyes held Nick's a long moment.

"You've got the look of your father," the colonel said finally, releasing his hand.

"So they tell me."

"You have his guts?"

"I doubt that, sir."

"Your service record says something very different. Vince must have been very proud of you, son."

There was nothing Nick could say in response to that. If his father had found his record a source of pride, he had never indicated it.

"Thank you, sir."

"I didn't know your father very well, Ms. Simonson," Kittering said, turning to Cara. "He arrived in country shortly before my tour was over. According to the DOA, he served honorably. May I express my condolences to you on his untimely death."

"Thank you," Cara said, extending her hand.

Kittering took it in both of his. "Terrible business this."

"Yes, it is. And Nick and I seem to have come to the end of our resources. We're hopeful that you and Mr. Ainsworth may be able to help us."

"I took the liberty of giving Colonel Kittering the list you showed me yesterday. I had hoped he might remember something—or some*one*—who can help us identify those remaining names."

"I don't believe I can live up to that advance billing," Kittering said. "Why don't we all sit down, and I'll tell you what I can."

There was something about the disclaimer that told Nick they weren't going to get the answers they needed. Not from Kittering. And obviously not from Ainsworth and the Bureau.

"You didn't recognize either of the nicknames?"

"The Shark and Buddy?" Kittering said, shaking his head. "Believe me, I've racked my brain, but I swear I don't remember anyone who was called by those names."

"Do you think it's possible—" Cara began.

"How about Johns in the company?" Nick broke in quickly.

He had had the feeling Cara was going to ask the colonel about the helicopter unit she'd discovered. Even if he doubted the connection, he would rather not reveal that information in front of Ainsworth. Not until he had decided exactly how much he could be trusted.

"Any who were close to my father?" he went on. "Someone who served in the same platoon perhaps?"

"There were several Johns in the company, but none of them in your father's platoon that I remember. Regrettably, both Lieutenant Stone and Staff Sergeant Misso were killed in action. I did contact Stone's replacement, who remembered your father, Ms. Simonson, but not the others. They were apparently gone before he arrived."

"So essentially you're telling us that there's no one from my father's platoon who might be able to identify these last three names?"

"No one I've been able to discover. I contacted a few people who were in the company during your father's time, including the first sergeant. Neither of those nicknames rang bells with him, but he did remind me of something that happened during that year. An incident that might possibly be related to what's going on."

"What kind of incident?"

"A fragging. Are you familiar with the term?" The last was addressed to Cara, who shook her head. "Mr. Morelli?"

Nick hadn't heard the word in years, but he knew what it meant. And he was aware that there had been several instances in Vietnam. Undoubtedly more than in any other combat the U.S. military had engaged in.

"An enlisted man kills his officer," he said, "usually by throwing a grenade into the tent while he's sleeping."

The culprit was seldom caught, even if others in the unit knew who he was. Fragging was normally reserved for an officer believed to be putting his unit in unnecessary danger because he was bucking for promotion. And doing so at the cost of the lives of his men.

If something like that had happened while his father had been in country, it wasn't surprising Nick hadn't been aware of it. Not given Vince Morelli's reticence about 'Nam.

"It happened more rarely than the public has been led to believe by movies and books about the war," Kittering continued, "but I'm sorry to say it *did* occur."

"And in *this* particular company?"

Kittering nodded. "The lieutenant who commanded the platoon before Stone. He wasn't liked, and I doubt many people grieved. The murderer was never charged."

"You think that has something to do with what's going on now?"

"It seems far-fetched to connect the two, I suppose, until you hear that the person almost everyone suspected of tossing that grenade was a private by the name of McGregor."

"Duncan McGregor?"

"I understand you believe he is one of the people on your father's list."

"Was," Nick said. "He was inside his cabin in Tennessee when it was blown up."

"Someone was inside," Ainsworth interjected.

"Are you suggesting—" Nick stopped the question he'd begun, thinking about the implications.

"I talked to the sheriff in Bassett County after the colonel told me that story. He confirmed that they have no way to identify the remains found in that fire. McGregor had no DNA on file. No dental records exist, at least as far as they've been able to discover. They're *assuming* it was McGregor because it was his cabin, but they have no proof."

"McGregor was one mean SOB," Kittering said. "I'm sorry, Ms. Simonson, but there is no other language to describe him. He was universally disliked. And, as I said, everyone in the company suspected he was responsible for the death of that officer."

"Is it possible that your father might have known something about that murder and have finally resolved to bring it to the attention of the authorities?" Ainsworth asked.

At this point, almost anything was possible, but somehow that didn't sound like his dad.

"Maybe," Nick conceded. "But if so, why now?"

"Have you checked his medical records?" Kittering asked. "Contacted his doctor? A newly awakened knowledge of his own mortality can make a man do all sorts of things. Maybe even decide to turn in a murderer."

"After thirty-five years?" Cara asked.

Kittering turned to smile at her. "Old men don't like the thought of going to their maker with stains on their souls, my dear. Soldiers already have enough of a burden to bear in that respect perhaps, but if Vince knew that someone had killed one of our own…" The colonel shrugged. "You knew your father better than I did, of course," he said, addressing the last remark to Nick. "What if he'd recently been given bad news about his health? Mightn't he have decided to start putting some things right in his life?"

Like the screwed-up relationship with his only son?

If so, Nick had seen no sign of that kind of effort at atonement.

"Which suggests he's the one who contacted Agent Crawford rather than vice versa. Is that what you've discovered?" Nick asked Ainsworth, ignoring the sympathy in Kittering's eyes.

"We haven't found anything relating to your father or Ms. Simonson's in Crawford's case files. There's nothing there that even tangentially touches on Vietnam."

"Maybe your dad didn't tell the special agent what he wanted to see him about," Kittering suggested.

"Would Crawford have arranged to fly down to meet my father without knowing what he wanted to talk about?"

"It's highly unlikely. There are budgetary restrictions we have to live by. Crawford would have had to have some assurance that the topic would be of interest to the Bureau."

"Would the fragging the colonel referred to be of interest to you?"

Cara's question went to the heart of Kittering's theory. Would the FBI have sent out an agent to investigate a wartime crime that had happened so long ago?

"There's no statute of limitations on murder, of course, but normally we would turn something like that over to the CID. Actually, I can't think of anything relating to Vietnam that we wouldn't have sent to Defense."

"So my theory comes to naught," Kittering said with a smile.

"Not necessarily," Ainsworth said. "It's just that as of right now, we don't seem to be able to make the pieces of the puzzle tie together. The McGregor angle is certainly one we should keep in mind."

"I take it that means the Bureau is going to pursue this."

The executive assistant director again looked surprised at Nick's question. "If it turns out that one of our agents died as a result of foul play in regards to this case, then you can be sure we'll pursue it, Mr. Morelli. And I'd suggest that right now you and Ms. Simonson should step back and let us do a job we are far better equipped to handle than the two of you."

"DO *YOU* THINK McGregor's still alive?" Cara asked as soon as they were in the corridor outside the office. "That *is* what Ainsworth was suggesting, wasn't it?"

"For some reason that seems to be what Ainsworth wants us to believe."

"To keep us from pursuing this any further?" Although he had couched it as a suggestion, Ainsworth had certainly warned them off at the end of the interview.

"Or to throw us off track."

"Which would mean that he knows what's going on."

"Well, he *does* have access to Crawford's files."

Nick didn't look at her as he said it. She had already given him her reasons for not wanting to prowl through the Bureau's database. If the FBI had become convinced that their agent's death wasn't from natural causes, then there would be a security alert on anything having to do with what he was working on. And if Ainsworth was covering up what that was, then the pertinent information had probably already been deleted.

"You think he's lying about there being nothing in them?"

"I think he's lying about something. I gave him an opportunity to make some sense of this, and he didn't take it."

"I don't understand."

"I asked him if Crawford would have flown down to meet with my father if he hadn't known what he wanted."

"And he said that given government budget constraints probably not. What's wrong with that?"

"If my dad had called the FBI, even going through the central switchboard here in Washington, they wouldn't have sent an agent from here to interview him."

"They would have sent someone from the local field office," Cara said, realizing what Nick was getting at. "You think that means the Bureau contacted him. And if they did, then Ainsworth must know why."

"Even if he didn't know at the time, I think he would by now. It was obvious from what he said that he had someone look through the case files."

"Maybe since Crawford hadn't done the interview yet, he hadn't created a file about your father's call."

"Then you're back to why an agent from Washington would fly down to Mississippi. If Crawford didn't know what my father wanted to talk about—and think it was important—then he would have passed the information on to the field office in Jackson."

"Maybe—"

She stopped so abruptly that Nick had taken a couple of steps past her before he realized she was no longer walking beside him. He turned back to find her standing in the middle of the hallway, her mouth still open from the sentence she hadn't completed.

"What?"

"Ainsworth said there was nothing relating to your father in the case files."

"That's right."

"But that's not the only kind of files the FBI handles," she said. "And the others aren't included in the database."

"The others?"

"Background checks. Security clearances. What if Crawford was asking too many questions? Or asking the wrong people?"

"You think *he* was the original target? Wouldn't that have set off alarm bells about the person whose clearance he was working on?"

"Not if he died of a heart attack," Cara said.

Apparently they had really believed that. At least in the beginning. If Crawford had been working on a background check, then either Cara's question or Nick's phone call or maybe the combination of the two had made the Bureau suspicious enough to ask her to come in.

Because they believed she knew more than she did? Or because they were genuinely trying to gather information about the death of one of their agents?

Ainsworth had warned them off, but that could be put down to nothing more than the Bureau's normal arrogance that they were better equipped to handle whatever was going on than a couple of outsiders. The meeting with Kittering and his suggestions about McGregor and the health of Nick's father had obviously been intended to give them something else to think about. Maybe even to deliberately throw them off the trail.

The trouble was they had lost the trail with McGregor's death. And unless Cara's long shot with the Sharks came through, Nick was again at a loss about what to do next.

"IT'S POSSIBLE CRAWFORD was working on a background check. Security clearance for some kind of office or appointment or confirmation. Maybe something high profile that my father might have seen in the newspaper or on TV," Nick said into the phone, remembering the battered recliner aligned with the screen. "He called the FBI on the tenth, so either that day or a day or so before. It may have taken him a few days to make up his mind to make that call."

He listened as Dalton repeated the pertinent information, making sure he'd gotten the dates right. Griff had offered the full resources of the Phoenix. Tracking Cara's idea down was something the agency was in a position to do far better than Nick could from this room.

Although he had made certain they weren't followed from the FBI building, he hadn't taken Cara back to the Wardman. He'd parked the Jeep in a long-term lot and then taken a cab to a motel on the outskirts of the city. He'd waited to make the call until he could give the Phoenix his exact location.

"Oh, and one more thing. Track down whatever information you can find on Lieutenant Colonel Ron Kittering." Nick spelled the last name. "He was the company commander at the time. He claims that a fragging incident took place in the battalion, which McGregor was widely suspected of carrying out. I'd like to know if it happened, as well as anything you can tell me about Kittering's activities since 'Nam."

As he listened to Dalton's recap of these instructions, Nick glanced over to the desk where Cara was setting up her laptop. Her expectation of an answer to her morning's e-mail was an even longer shot than that something would come of the things he had just asked the Phoenix to check out.

"That's it," he confirmed when Rawls had finished. "Anything turn up I should know about?"

"Nothing on this end. We're still trying to locate members of your father's platoon. I'll get started on these two angles right away."

"Okay, let me know if you get any interesting results on either."

He pushed the off button on the phone and walked over to where Cara was in the process of connecting to the Internet. He watched over her shoulder as the "check mail" icon came up, preparing to comfort her disappointment.

There were several messages, but her cursor tracked immediately to the third one, which he realized must be from an address she didn't recognize. She opened it, apparently reading the text much faster than he was.

"This is it," she said, her voice tinged with disbelief, just as the sense of the unsigned words on the screen made it into his consciousness.

Jack Davis can tell you about the incident you're seeking. Davis Air Freight. Shula, Louisiana.

Chapter Twenty

Shula, Louisiana

"Jack Davis?"

The white-haired man standing on the tarmac of the small regional airport glanced in their direction, his eyes narrowed against the glare of the afternoon sun. "Who wants to know?"

He signed the paper on the clipboard he was holding and then handed it to a young man dressed in jeans and a T-shirt, who had been waiting for it. The kid started toward a nearby hangar, the clipboard in one hand and a bulky package under the other arm. Only then did Davis turn to face them.

"Nick Morelli," Nick said. He walked through the flight line exit of the small, independent airfreight office that had Davis's name over the front door, his hand extended.

"I know you?" Davis asked.

"No, sir."

"You got something that needs to be flown out to the rigs?"

Apparently most of Davis's airfreight business dealt with the delivery of packages to the oil rigs scattered along the Louisiana coastline.

"No, I don't. I need to talk to you—"

"Son, I got a business to run here. I don't have time for talking. If you aren't a customer, then you need to get off my strip."

Nick ignored the interruption, although Davis had already turned toward the hangar where the kid had disappeared. Inside it sat an old Huey. Like Davis, the chopper looked as if it had been through the wars.

"—about something that happened in early November of 1968, somewhere in I-Corps," Nick went on, raising his voice so that it would carry across the distance Davis's hurried gait had opened between them. "Something I think you have information about."

Stopping in midstride, the pilot swung around to face him. Nick was close enough now to see that the narrowed eyes peering at him were blue. Although the color was faded, their gaze was as direct as an arrow. The thin lips beneath the long, hooked nose pursed as the older man studied him.

"I been waiting thirty-five years for somebody to walk through my door and ask me about that," he said finally, still ignoring Nick's outstretched hand. "Why you? And why the hell now?"

"Because whatever happened back then, someone killed my father to keep him from talking about it."

The blue eyes widened a little, and then Davis nodded. "I can see the resemblance. Morelli, you say?"

"You didn't know him?"

"Your dad? Only saw him that once. I used to wonder what happened to him, but I knew they wouldn't like me trying to find out."

"They?" Cara asked.

The pilot's eyes considered her a moment. "Now don't tell me you're his daughter. Not with that hair."

Cara smiled at him. "No, but my father was there that day. Hiram Simonson."

It seemed to Nick that she said it almost hopefully, but Davis shook his head.

"I didn't know any of their names. I didn't *want* to. The only reason I talked to Morelli was because I thought they'd done it. And because I knew there was going to be hell to pay."

"You thought they'd done what?" Nick asked carefully.

He wasn't going to try to convince this man that they knew more than they did. His gut instinct was that Jack Davis was a straight shooter. They probably had one chance to get him to talk about what happened that day, and that was to be absolutely honest. Both about their lack of knowledge and their motives in coming here. And after all, it was to Davis's advantage to listen to them as much as it was to their advantage to hear whatever it was he'd waited thirty-five years to tell somebody.

"You don't know?" Davis asked, bushy white brows arching in surprise.

"What I know is that three of the men who were there that day are dead. Along with an FBI agent who was investigating it. They were killed because they saw whatever you saw. The odds are good you're the next person on the list of people to be taken out because you know what those three men knew. In order to put a stop to the killings—and to protect your own life—you need to tell us what it is that someone is so determined to prevent becoming public knowledge."

"Is that what they did? Your dad and the others? Threaten to go public?"

"I don't know. All I know is that my father had an appointment with an FBI agent and both of them were murdered. As were Cara's father and a man named Duncan McGregor." He waited a moment, giving Davis time to react to the name, but the pilot shook his head. "They were on a list of names my father wrote down in preparation for his meeting with the FBI special agent. There were three other names on that list. John, Buddy and The Shark. We didn't know until a few hours ago that Shark wasn't a nickname."

"And you tracked me down from *that?* Hell, the FBI needs to hire you."

"We found you with the anonymous help of someone on your unit's Listserv. He suggested that you might know what we were looking for."

"That son of a bitch," Davis said vehemently.

"Whoever he is," Nick said, "he may have saved your life."

"Or he may have led them right to me. Just like he did you."

Nick couldn't deny the reality of that. It seemed that every scrap of information they found, the killers had gotten there ahead of them. He had actually been shocked to find Davis still alive.

"I don't see how," Nick assured him. "That e-mail was a private communication. He just said we should talk to you."

"You shoulda talked to *him*. Bastard saw the same thing I did. Gotta be the slick," Davis muttered the words almost to himself. "Gilbert was the other gun that day, and he went down at An Loc."

"The other gun?"

"Gunship," Davis explained, glancing back at Cara when she asked her question. "Helicopter gunship," he added. "And I'll save you the trouble. Slicks were the ones *without* guns."

"So you think the pilot of the slick is the one who e-mailed me?" she asked, apparently having no trouble absorbing the unfamiliar terminology.

"Got to be. *If* it was someone on the Listserv like he said." He nodded toward Nick.

"So why wouldn't he just talk to us himself? Why send us to you?"

"'Cause we were all told *not* to talk. And maybe because I was the team lead that day," Davis added grudgingly.

"Who told you not to talk?" Nick asked, drawing the pilot's attention back to him.

"Word came down the chain of command."

"So you *did* report what happened?"

"You bet your ass I did. They weren't hanging that shit on us. Your dad felt the same way."

"That he was going to be blamed for it?"

"Hell, I did at first. Blamed his team that is. And when he told me what really happened…"

The words faded. Davis's eyes focused on the battered helicopter, but it was obvious that wasn't what he was seeing. He was lost in the past, thinking about whatever had set off the chain of events that had brought them here today.

"That's what we need to know, Mr. Davis," Cara reminded him softly. "We need you to tell us exactly what happened that day."

"We were headed back to Duc Pho anyway, so they told us to gather up the new meat and take 'em with us. There wasn't but one kid that day, green as grass and looking like he was gonna puke as soon as we took off. About halfway there, we got a call to divert to fly cover for a slick picking up a LRRP team."

"Lurp?" Cara repeated his pronunciation of the unfamiliar acronym.

"Long Range Reconnaissance Patrol. Four guys who got sent out to survey the lay of the land. They operated away from base for days, sometimes weeks, and then somebody would pick them up and bring them in for debriefing. There was nothing unusual about the request to cover the operation. As I said, we were headed home anyway."

Davis had taken them into his crowded office, which looked out on the hangar and the airstrip his air-freight operation used. He offered Cara the only chair, and then cleared the clutter off one side of his desk for Nick to perch on.

When Nick declined, preferring to stand, Davis sat there himself. His fingers played with an old Zippo lighter as he talked, clicking the lid up and down.

"The team we were to pick up was supposed to lay down smoke to guide us in. When we got to the coordinates, I see the signal smoke go up. We head toward it, low leveling, and suddenly down below us is this village."

For a long moment Davis's eyes lost focus as they had outside on the tarmac. The memory of whatever had happened that day was apparently still vivid enough to cause him to see it over and over again.

"Except there wasn't a soul alive down there," he said. "The bodies were piled in the middle like so much cordwood. Women, kids, old people. They were all there. I don't know if they'd shot the dogs, but none of them were around. That in itself was weird enough. Those mutts were always there in any Vietnamese village. All of 'em yapping. Dozens of them. Here…here there was nothing. Not one living soul."

This, then, was what they had come to hear. This was the outrage that had cost at least four men—and maybe more—their lives.

And despite the long years that had passed, there was something so powerful about the recitation that for seemingly endless minutes no one said a word. It was Davis who finally broke the silence.

"This wasn't a hot zone, you understand. Not a village identified as sympathetic to the Cong. It was just…" Davis took another deep breath before he went on, leaving the rest of his description unspoken. "I thought the LRRP team had done it, and then just called us in to pick them up, putting us right smack in the middle of that shit. I was so furious my hand was shaking on the stick. I remember that nobody in the flight was saying anything. We were all just hovering over that god-awful mound of bodies.

"Finally I said to Gilbert that we needed to get the hell out of there. It was obvious there was no one down there who needed our help. By then I was wondering if this was what the team had been sent here to do. If they'd been ordered to wipe out the village. I know that sounds…" He glanced up, maybe to read their reaction. "It was war. A kind this country had never fought before. Stranger things happened in that hellhole."

The sickness that had been growing in Nick's stomach suddenly escalated. Was this what had changed his father into the cold, unfeeling bastard he'd been?

"Is that what had happened?" Cara asked.

Those were words Nick couldn't have enunciated at this moment if his life had depended on it. He didn't even want to think about his father taking part in the massacre of women and children that Davis had just described.

Nick had killed men, and not only in combat. As a Ranger, he'd been taught a dozen ways to take a life with his bare hands. But this was something different. This was something United States soldiers didn't do.

"I wanted to see the bastard who had ordered that," Davis said. "Even though I knew I might get court-martialed for doing it, I sat those Hueys down almost on top of those guys. One look at their faces, and I figured I'd been right. LRRPs were no pussies, believe me, but those guys were ashen. I was outta that bird screaming at the sergeant before the rotor stopped. I didn't get half a dozen words out of my mouth before he starts screaming back."

The sergeant. Sergeant Morelli. That was exactly how his father had identified himself to Crawford, Nick remembered. *Because that's who he had been when all this had gone down.*

"Screaming what?" Nick forced himself to ask.

"That it wasn't them. I didn't believe him at first, but he kept yelling that they hadn't had anything to do with it. I kept yelling back at him, 'Then who the hell did?' It took a while for both of us to calm down enough for me to make any sense out of what he was saying.

"They heard the shooting—clearly from American weapons—so they moved in close enough to see what was going on. When they got there, right in the middle of the village is this blue-and-white chopper. It wasn't marked, but we all knew who those birds belonged to," Davis said with a trace of bitterness.

"Air America," Nick supplied, feeling another piece of the puzzle slip into place.

"Bingo. Your dad knew immediately that whatever was going on inside the village was a CIA operation.

There were four or five of them. No insignias on the uniforms they wore. Nothing to identify them."

Davis paused, glancing again at Cara as if concerned about the effect on her of what he was about to relate. No matter how gruesome it was, she had a right to hear it, Nick thought. What had happened that day had cost her father his life.

"Go on," Nick urged.

The chill in the pit of his stomach had begun to dissipate. Whatever had been done to that village, his father apparently hadn't been involved. As bad as he suspected the rest of this was going to be, that knowledge would allow him to listen to it dispassionately.

At this point, all he wanted from Davis was to understand how this incident was tied to the deaths of the men on his father's list and why the FBI had gotten involved.

"The guy in charge was wearing a frigging cowboy hat, if you can believe it." The contempt in Davis's voice was clear and cold. "He was letting one of the others do the questioning, but he was the one doing all the shooting. Nice and neat, too. Execution style. They ask the question, and when he didn't get the answer he wanted, he put his pistol to the temple of whichever poor SOB he'd picked out and pulled the trigger."

It was an image already associated in the minds of many with that war. There was probably not an American from that era who didn't know that those kinds of executions had taken place. Nick certainly did.

And he had spent enough years with the Agency and on the External Security Team to understand that the assassination of one madman can prevent the deaths of countless innocents. It didn't sound as if that was what this had been.

"And they killed them all?" Cara asked, her voice touched with the horror anyone with normal sensibilities would feel at Davis's description.

"What were they asking them?" Nick interrupted before Davis answered.

Was there any question that would have justified that massacre? Were the lives of American soldiers at stake? Was this village an unidentified stronghold of Cong support?

"None of your dad's team was fluent enough in Vietnamese to understand everything, but they understood enough to know what the Air America boys wanted, though. Especially the cowboy. He said it over and over again. It was a word we'd all heard. At least enough to understand what it meant.

"They were asking about heroin. They had come there to pick it up in that big old Air America chopper and found that the shipment they were expecting wasn't there. Somebody else had taken it. Maybe the village elders had sold it to a higher bidder. Maybe the Cong had gotten wind of it and raided the place. Or the ARVN. Who knows what the hell happened? And it didn't matter. The fact that they no longer had it pissed old Cowboy Bob off enough that he was taking no prisoners. They kept asking the question and since no one could give 'em the right answer, they all ended up dead."

It was exactly the kind of thing that someone would kill to keep from coming to light. Someone associated with the Agency might conceivably be able to explain away the deaths of a village full of noncombatants, especially in a guerilla war like 'Nam. Explaining away the fact that those deaths had been inflicted because of a drug deal gone bad would be another story entirely.

"You know who he was?"

"The cowboy?" Davis asked, shaking his head. "I told you. No one was wearing any insignia. They certainly weren't wearing name tags."

Which meant they were almost back where they'd started. They now knew what had happened, but Davis's testimony was secondhand information. He hadn't personally seen the massacre.

What he knew was enough to make him a target, just as Cara's father had been, but it wasn't enough to convict anyone. Not in a court of law. A consideration that was moot right now, Nick conceded, since they were no closer to knowing the name of the CIA operative who had carried out that slaughter.

"But I'd know him if I ever saw him again."

Davis's claim was as unexpected as it was baffling. If he hadn't seen the attack on the village, then how could he possibly hope to identify the perpetrator?

"They were still there when you arrived?" Nick asked. It seemed the only explanation.

"Long gone. But the bastards were refueling at Duc Pho when we got back. Bigger 'an Dixie. Same blue-and-white chopper the sergeant had described. Same asshole in charge. Same frigging cowboy hat."

"And you saw him?"

Nick couldn't control the flood of excitement that realization produced. Maybe Davis hadn't seen the killings, but he had seen the man who had carried them out. And if he really could identify him—

The door to the office opened, admitting the same young man they'd seen outside with the clipboard. He didn't even look their way, simply holding out whatever paperwork he needed a signature on to Davis.

The pilot slid off the edge of the desk, turning toward the door. Without comment, he took the board and scrawled his name across the bottom of the form before returning it to the kid, who held another package in his other hand.

As he walked back toward the open door, Davis seemed to be peering beyond it. He took a step closer, tilting his head to see around the departing kid.

"Who's in the hangar?"

Surprised, the boy turned back to face his boss before his gaze followed Davis's toward the chopper. "Said he was with the maintenance company."

"Maintenance? Doing what kind of maintenance?"

The kid shrugged, looking blank.

"We got no maintenance scheduled this week. Those bastards just want to work up something they can bill me for."

Pushing past the boy, Davis burst from the office, starting across the tarmac at a jog. "Hey! Hey, you! What the hell do you think you're doing to my bird?"

The heavyset man who was bent over the raised engine cowling lifted his head, looking toward the office. He turned to face the approaching pilot, but he didn't move away from the helicopter. Instead he began to reach inside the partially unzipped mechanic's coverall he was wearing.

Nick had followed Davis to the door of the office, looking across the brilliant afternoon sunshine into the shadowed hangar. As soon as he saw the man's hand dip inside his clothing, he knew what was about to happen.

As if the action were unfolding in slow motion, he watched the hand come back into sight, and this time it wasn't empty. The handgun he was holding was large—even at this distance incredibly menacing.

As the mechanic wrapped both hands around the weapon's grip, raising it to sight along the long barrel, Nick pulled his semiautomatic from the holster he wore beneath his blazer. He sprinted toward the white-haired man striding angrily across the narrow airstrip.

"Get down!" he screamed, taking aim at the man in the hangar. "Davis, get down!"

The report of the mechanic's gun seemed to echo inside the cavernous building, reverberating through the metal structure like thunder. Jack Davis's body jerked, as if his forward progress had been stopped by shock or surprise.

Nick's return shot missed as the mechanic ducked under the chopper. He heard it ping off something metallic.

By that time Nick had reached Davis. The pilot had both hands pressed over his right side, looking down at the blood pouring out between his fingers. Nick supported him as his body slid down awkwardly until he was sitting on the asphalt, still holding his side.

"That son of a bitch shot me." The words were gasped as Davis looked up at Nick, the faded blue eyes wide with shock. "Son of a *bitch*." The last word held the same note of surprise reflected in his gaze.

Behind them, Nick could hear Cara's running footsteps. "Call 911." He threw the order over his shoulder. "And stay with him."

"Where are *you* going?" she asked, stooping to take his place beside the wounded man. She had already begun fumbling in her purse for her cell phone.

"After him," Nick said, nodding toward the fleeing figure of the fake mechanic, who was running across the wide-open expanse of runway toward the distant airport fence.

Chapter Twenty-One

It didn't take but a quick glance across the airport as Nick ran to understand where the mechanic was headed. Beyond the perimeter security fence a black car was parked. The windows were tinted so that he couldn't tell if there was an accomplice inside.

Just at that moment the man in the coveralls turned, slowing to point his weapon at Nick. He'd have to be a hell of a shot to make that one on the run, Nick thought, but the guy *had* managed to hit Davis.

Nick began to zigzag, knowing the evasion would slow him down, but so would a 9mm slug. The shooter got off a couple of rounds before he decided to cut his losses and again headed at full speed toward the fence and the waiting car. Nick didn't waste time aiming at the runner. The distance was too great for success.

The man had gotten a good head start when Nick had stopped to see about Davis. Unless he could somehow make up the difference...

He increased his speed, no longer forced to dodge bullets. By now, the mechanic was scrambling up the security fence and not making a particularly effective job of it. Either he was as out of shape as he looked or his hands were sweaty. He made it about halfway up before his fingers slipped off the wire, causing him to tumble back onto the asphalt.

Seeing his fall sent adrenaline roaring through Nick's veins. He could catch this bastard. Or at least he could get near enough to put a bullet into him before he could scale the fence again.

Of course, the latter option posed the unwanted possibility that he might kill the man he was pursuing, no matter where he aimed. The ammo he was using could do considerable damage, maybe even enough that he would bleed to death before the paramedics arrived. And he needed to be able to answer questions about whoever had set all this into motion.

Besides, with the guy's renewed struggle to get over the fence, Nick was gaining on him. He might not be forced to use a bullet to stop him.

At that moment the driver's side door of the black car opened. Apparently the mechanic's accomplice had just realized the same thing.

Running full-out, his breath sawing in and out in hard-won gasps, Nick knew the odds were about to change. And whoever was joining the party wasn't going to be hampered by having to climb over that expanse of chain-link fencing.

He debated skidding to a stop and taking his best shot. Of course, the possibility that then there would be no one left to answer questions was still a consideration. And he couldn't decide which one he should target first in hopes of being able to physically collar the other.

In all likelihood the one who had stayed in the car would be higher on the food chain than the man sent in to tamper with Davis's engine. Did that mean he would also be more knowledgeable about the man behind the murders?

Even if that were the case, he was on the other side of the fence with quick access to a means of escape. And he was also sighting down the barrel of a gun that looked every bit as menacing as the mechanic's.

Nick began to swerve again, firing back in an attempt to keep the shooter honest. The window behind the driver shattered, forcing him to retreat to the other side of the car.

By now Nick was almost to the fence. The guy who had shot Davis had reached the top, but his feet were still within reach. Nick fired again, aiming at the car in an attempt to force the man who had been driving to keep his head down for a few seconds.

Then he reached up, grasping the climber by an ankle. The mechanic shook his foot, trying to break the hold that was preventing him from getting over the fence.

"Get down," Nick demanded, pointing the Glock upward in the general vicinity of the guy's privates. "Get down now or I swear I'll blow them off."

The mechanic looked down, his eyes widening with the realization of the threat he faced. Nick flicked a quick glance at the second man. The one who was supposed to be cowering behind the car. He was again sighting along the barrel of his gun, which was pointed directly at Nick.

In an automatic reflex action Nick swung the Glock in that direction, getting off a shot that made the man taking aim at him duck down behind the car again. Before he could redirect his attention to the man on the fence, the mechanic turned loose, landing directly on top of Nick.

It felt like someone had just slammed a baseball bat into his damaged ribs. The Glock hit the ground before Nick and the guy on top of him did. Trying not to pass out from the agonizing pain in his side, Nick was aware of his gun skittering away across the tarmac.

Reacting with an instinct driven by both self-preservation and the years of training, he was able to get his left hand wrapped around the mechanic's right wrist, forcing the gun he held up and away from his forehead. With his other hand, Nick fended off his assailant's attempt to get his other hand around Nick's throat. The struggle for control of the weapon seemed to go on for an eternity, but during those endless seconds neither of them said a word.

Sweat beaded the red, straining face of the mechanic. His lips were drawn back from his teeth like a death mask, the teeth themselves locked together as he fought to free his arm from Nick's grasp.

Nick had no idea what the second man was doing, but at least he wasn't shooting at them. Not yet.

Maybe he was afraid of hitting his partner. Or maybe he trusted that, given the mechanic's considerable bulk, he would succeed in subduing Nick without his intervention.

In the distance, faintly, he heard the low wail of a siren. Apparently the emergency system had responded to Cara's call. And if there was a God in heaven, along with the paramedics would come a representative of the county's law enforcement agency. *Please, God.*

The sound of reinforcements seemed to pump new strength into his muscles. Instead of simply trying to keep the muzzle of the gun from coming in contact with his forehead again, Nick attempted to wrest it from his opponent's hands.

As they struggled, Nick gradually became aware of another sound. One that was much nearer than the sirens. One he had heard only minutes before and had immediately recognized. Just as he recognized them now.

Cara's footsteps.

Seemingly without his conscious volition, he turned his head, desperate to locate her, despite the life-and-death struggle he was engaged in. As he did, the thick wrist he'd been holding turned within his fingers. He could feel his grip begin to slide against the sweat-slicked skin.

His eyes rose to the florid face above him. The feral grin widened as if in triumph.

If the man managed to pull his arm free, as it seemed likely he would, not only would he be able to turn the gun he held on Nick, but he could also then direct it toward the woman running across the runway.

And there was no way in hell Nick was going to let that happen.

With a surge of strength for which there was no rational explanation, Nick regained control of the wrist that had been slipping away from him. Then, with a force fueled by that same fear, he jerked downward and to his right, slamming the knuckles of the man who held the gun onto the pavement. He was rewarded by a howl of pain and a profanity.

Before those had died away, Nick slammed the man's hand against the asphalt again. At the same time, he strained to roll his body to the right in an attempt to dislodge the man on top of him.

His assailant countered the move by throwing his entire weight in the opposite direction. Locked together, the sheer bulk of the other man's body carried

Nick with it, so that for an instant Nick was facing the fence.

Once more the man who'd been waiting behind it was aligning his weapon for a shot. Apparently he had discounted any threat from Cara. Like a malevolent eye, the dark hole of the muzzle was tracking the movements of the two men on the ground.

Using the momentum generated by the bigger man's movement, Nick continued their roll in the direction of the black car, putting the mechanic between himself and the man aiming the pistol. He felt the impact of the bullet as it tore into the mechanic's flesh before he heard the report of the gun. Then came the echo, which sounded almost on top of the shot.

Except here in the open, there should be no echo, he realized. It wasn't until the man who'd been standing behind the black car fell face forward onto its hood, however, that Nick understood what he had heard had not been an echo, but a second shot.

He pushed the body of the mechanic who'd taken the bullet, away from him. The man was obviously still alive, his breath coming in sobs, punctuated periodically by a low moan.

Although it would be a bonus if he could live long enough to be questioned, right now Nick didn't give a damn whether or not he did. Right now...

He turned his head and saw Cara kneeling on the asphalt. For an instant he thought she, too, had been shot. Then he saw that she was holding his Glock out in front of her in both hands, the muzzle still pointed in the direction of the fence and the black car.

Beyond her, an emergency vehicle screeched to a halt beside the fallen pilot. Two men jumped out of the truck almost before it had come to a stop.

There was no accompanying cop car, however, as Nick had hoped. No policeman with his weapon drawn.

Nick's gaze returned to the woman kneeling between him and the paramedics. He hadn't been wrong. She was the only one who could have taken out the accomplice.

"Nick? Are you all right?"

He wasn't, he realized belatedly. His lungs felt as if drawing the next breath was a challenge. Only now that it was over was he fully aware of the results of having two hundred and fifty pounds dropped on him from a height of eight feet.

His ribs were screaming. His right shoulder, which had slammed into the asphalt first, seemed to be joining in the chorus.

None of that mattered right now. The only thing that mattered…

He began to try to get up. He got his right hand under him enough to propel his body into a sitting position. Getting from there to his knees was relatively easy, despite the protest from his ribs. Standing was a far greater challenge because by this time his legs had begun to tremble in reaction.

By the time he had managed it, Cara was also on her feet. She still held the gun in both hands, but it was no longer pointed at the man sprawled across the hood of the car.

"What the hell did I tell you?"

Her eyes widened at his tone, but she didn't retreat as he approached her. His fury was so strong it crowded his throat, making it difficult to enunciate any of the things he wanted to say to her.

"Answer me, damn it. What did I tell you?"

She shook her head, her eyes holding his. Her left

hand released its hold on the semiautomatic, allowing her arms to fall to her sides.

She had just saved his life, and he was yelling at her. There was no way she could know what those few seconds when he'd heard her running toward that gun had done to him. And instead of the disaster he'd envisioned...

"And who the *hell* taught you to shoot like that?"

He was standing in front of her now, looking down into her face. He had forgotten how clear her skin was. Almost transparent in the sunlight.

The wind blew a strand of hair across her cheek. She raised her hand, still holding his eyes as she brushed it away. Hers were almost defiant.

"My father taught me. He had wanted a son, but I was what he got. Maybe he was disappointed, but... He taught me to handle a gun. Just like your dad taught you."

His father had never taught him anything, especially not how to shoot, but he didn't tell her that. Actually, he couldn't have told her if he'd wanted to because his throat was so tight with relief and love that it ached. Instead, he put his hands on her shoulders, realizing for the first time that the knuckles of the left were bleeding.

"Nick?"

"It's okay," he said, fighting for control. The last few minutes had been a roller coaster of emotions, but they were both alive. "I didn't mean to yell at you. I thought..."

You were going to be shot. That I was going to lose you. That before I'd had a chance to tell you any of the things I need to tell you, that you, too, were going to be snatched away from me.

230 Rules of Engagement

Instead of saying any of those things, he pulled her to him. Her eyes widened again, and then, as his mouth descended, they closed, her lashes falling to hide the anxiety that had been in them. She melted against him, her mouth opening at the first touch of his tongue to her lips.

Her arms lifted to lock around his neck, carrying the Glock with them. He could feel it against his back. For perhaps fifteen seconds he allowed himself to relish the fact that they were both unharmed and that despite the way his fear had caused him to act, she had still come willingly into his arms again. Then he broke the kiss, raising his head to look down into her face.

"Hold that thought, okay," he instructed softly.

And was rewarded by a lift at the corners of her mouth. She nodded, releasing her hold around his neck and stepping back. She turned, looking toward the paramedics who were working over Jack Davis.

"There's another couple who need attention over here," Nick yelled to them.

The wind whipped the words away, so that neither of the men moved. Nick put his hand in the small of Cara's back, directing her toward the hangar.

"I think he'd dead," she said, glancing up at him as they walked.

"Davis?"

There was a sick jolt of regret in the bottom of his stomach. The injury to the pilot had seemed to be low enough to have missed any vital organs, but just as he'd thought before, there was no way to gauge the damage a bullet could ultimately do, no matter where it struck.

"The man behind the car," Cara said. "I think I killed him."

He looked down into those clear blue eyes again and knew that she was seeking reassurance. He could still remember the first time he'd killed someone. It had been in combat, but that hadn't made the feeling any less disturbing.

"If you hadn't killed him, he would have shot both of us."

At least he would have shot Cara. There was no way he would have continued to negate the threat she posed once she'd pulled that trigger.

"I know. It's just…" She turned, looking toward Davis and the men working over him. "I've never done anything like that before. We shot skeet. Tin cans. I didn't think about him as a person—"

"Then don't think about it now," Nick said. "He was in on the murder of at least four men, including your father. If anybody ever deserved shooting…"

He let the rest of the sentence fade, knowing that this was a battle she'd have to fight. He'd told her the truth, and it ought to be enough. They had started this to *save* lives. Men like Jack Davis. Men who didn't deserve to die for what they had seen in a jungle thirty-five years ago. Men who had had no part in that massacre.

"There are two more by the fence," he said again, pitching his voice to carry to the paramedics. This time they looked up, their faces expressing their surprise. "How is he?"

"We'll know more when we get him to the hospital. How bad are the others?" the medic asked, getting to his feet.

"You should probably call for backup," Nick advised. "*And* the local authorities."

The young paramedic held his eyes for a moment

before his gaze focused on the Glock Nick had taken out of Cara's hands as they walked.

"You shoot him?" he asked, looking down at Davis.

"They did."

"You...a cop or something?"

"Something," Nick said, deciding that he'd prefer to make his explanations to the sheriff. "The guy on this side of the fence was still alive a minute or so ago. It would be good if we could keep him that way. He's got a lot of questions to answer."

The paramedic didn't move, his eyes clearly assessing Nick and the story. Finally he bent to fold up the medical supply box they'd been using to treat Davis's wound.

"Call for backup," he ordered his partner, and then, metal case in hand, he sprinted for the fence and the wounded mechanic.

Chapter Twenty-Two

"That son of a bitch," Jack Davis said softly, the picture Griff had just given him held in the hand that wasn't connected to a monitor.

The pilot's tanned face and blue eyes were a stark contrast to the crisp whiteness of the hospital pillows stacked behind him. Although he had been moved into a private room this morning, they had still had to get permission for the four of them to bring him the news.

"Someone you recognize, then" Nick said.

"Damn straight. It's Cowboy Bob all right. I told you'd I'd know him if I saw him again. Who is this bastard?"

"Randolph Streeter," Griff said. "Originally from San Antonio. A resident of the Beltway for the last thirty years."

"And someone one of the presidential candidates was considering for Secretary of Defense," Ainsworth added.

"*Was* considering?" Davis repeated, looking up at the FBI assistant executive director.

"Some difficulty with his clearances will undoubtedly prevent that," Ainsworth said.

"And nobody thought to check this guy's record before now?" The pilot's tone reflected his disgust with a process that would allow someone like Streeter to potentially reach that level of government service.

"The only thing his record reflected was his years of service with the CIA. Normally the Agency is hesitant to reveal where or how their operatives were employed, even years after the fact."

"So you're saying that if it wasn't for Morelli here, he might have actually made it?"

"If not for my father," Nick corrected. "He was the one who recognized Streeter from the newscasts and attempted to notify the Bureau about the incident in Vietnam."

"Which apparently threw Streeter into panic mode," Griff offered. "He'd come too far to let something he'd thought was well buried in the past come back to haunt him now."

"And once his cover started to unravel with Sergeant Morelli's phone call, he decided to make sure no one else got in the way of his ambitions," Ainsworth added. "It had been rumored that the position he was lobbying for was to be a stepping stone to the presidency."

"Now that's one hell of a scary proposition," Davis said, handing the old photograph back to Griff. "What I don't understand is how he ever found out about Morelli's call."

There was an awkward silence. The Phoenix contingent in the room was obviously not going to answer the question, and it was equally obvious the executive assistant director didn't want to.

"Mr. Streeter is an extremely wealthy individual," he said finally. "Apparently he had convinced someone inside the Bureau to pass along any information discovered during the background check Special Agent Crawford was conducting."

"He bribed them?"

"In this particular case it seemed to be a combination of bribery and blackmail. However, the kind of wealth Mr. Streeter has can buy a lot of eyes and ears. We're continuing our internal investigation to ensure that the person who was feeding him information is the only one who was on his payroll. And I can assure you that the guilty party will be prosecuted to the fullest extent of the law."

"It seems to me that whoever that was is as guilty of murder as the men who carried out Streeter's orders to kill."

After Cara's quiet comment, Ainsworth's discomfort was again evident. He made no attempt, however, to dodge the Bureau's responsibility for the leak.

"As I said, Ms. Simonson, he'll be punished to the fullest extent of the law."

"I think there's more than enough blame to go around," Griff said, stepping into the tension Ainsworth's confession had created. "I can assure you that Streeter's activities in Vietnam are an embarrassment to the Agency, as well. My wife's grandfather, who was the DCI at that time, would never condone that kind of behavior from one of his operatives."

"Is that how Streeter got to be 'extremely' wealthy?" Davis asked. "By doing a little drug-running using taxpayer financed Air America aircraft?"

"It's entirely possible that the foundation for his wealth was created at that time," Griff acknowledged. "He came home and invested heavily in the then booming oil industry in his home state. And whatever else he was, he was a shrewd investor, diversifying as the markets changed. His carefully cultivated contacts in government assured that his companies did very well in acquiring defense contracts, too."

"Maybe he had insider information to help him with those, as well," Cara suggested.

"There's no denying Streeter was well connected," Griff said. "He made friends in all the right places. He used his service with the CIA to open some doors that, given his origins, money alone might not have accomplished. Thanks to the three of you, however, the truth about all of that will now come out."

"It's gonna be hard to get a conviction for what he did as a spook in Southeast Asia so many years ago," Davis said. "A lot of people have already written off everyone involved in that war as dirty. He'll just be one more Ugly American. Besides, two of the men who actually saw him pull the trigger are dead."

"Three of them," Nick corrected. "John Terrell committed suicide twelve years ago. With the information you provided we've been able to determine he was the third man on that LRRP team. We haven't been able to locate Wilford Reynolds."

"Wilford?" Davis repeated the name, eyebrows raised.

"Nicknamed Buddy in childhood. We're still trying to find a current address."

"Even if we don't," Griff said, "the man who posed as a mechanic has decided to cooperate. He claims he had no part in the murders. He was hired because he knew enough about helicopter engines to sabotage one. He claims he panicked when you caught him at it."

"Son of a bitch didn't look particularly panicked when he pulled that trigger," Davis said.

"Still, it's a good trade-off," Cabot assured him. "The authorities have agreed to a lesser charge in exchange for his testimony against the man who hired him."

"Who, in turn, led us straight back to Streeter," Ainsworth added. "He may never be held accountable for that massacre in Vietnam, but I promise you he *will* be charged with the deaths of the men he killed to cover it up."

"So how did he get to me?" Davis asked. "I know how these two found me, but how did Streeter's goons get my name?"

"Streeter, having spent time in that area of Vietnam, would probably have known at once what Vince Morelli's reference 'The Shark' meant," Griff said. "And he was also at an advantage because he knew the approximate, if not the exact, date of the incident. All he had to do was have someone research the after-action reports of the missions the unit flew that day."

"You and my father both reported the incident up the chain of command," Nick said. "There would have to be records of those reports somewhere."

"So this guy's got flunkies leaking classified information to him from both the FBI *and* the DOA? Is that what you're telling me?"

Davis sounded as angry as Nick had been when he'd discovered how deeply entrenched Streeter's tentacles were in both intelligence services, as well as at the Department of Defense. Of course, as Ainsworth had already acknowledged, the kind of money Streeter had bought a lot of eyes and ears. And it was possible that the people who passed on information didn't understand the ramifications of what would be done with it.

"Was Kittering involved?" Nick asked.

It was something he hadn't thought to clarify before, but if his father had reported the incident as he told Davis he would, it would have been to his company commander. And the instructions to keep quiet about it, which Davis said he had received, would also have come down through Kittering. Nick had also been suspicious of the story the colonel told about the supposed fragging.

"There's no indication he was. McGregor *was* a suspect in the officer's death the colonel mentioned," Ainsworth said. "And besides, it was policy at the time that the military kept their noses out of what the Agency was doing. Streeter was in charge of operations in I-Corps. If the reports about the massacre had come to him, he would simply have instructed his military counterparts that what had happened at that village was a legitimate strike at the enemy. And he would probably have been believed. Maybe that's what Kittering was told. If he believed it, then he might still think the incident should be considered a legitimate operation, despite the questions you raised. Some men consider it an act of honor not to talk about something they were ordered not to talk about."

"And some men, like his dad," Davis said, nodding toward Nick, "consider it an act of honor to know when to tell the truth."

"Of course," Ainsworth said quickly. "I meant no disrespect to Sergeant Morelli. He saw a man he considered a war criminal being touted for a position of responsibility in the government. It took a great deal of courage to come forward and try to stop it, as respected as Streeter had become. And there was always the danger that he wouldn't be believed."

"Which makes me wonder why Streeter risked all this to keep my father from telling his story? Why didn't he just deny it had ever happened?"

"Maybe he risked it because he thought he was both powerful enough and smart enough to get away with it," Griff said. "An egomania that had been unchecked for more than thirty years. After all, the only people who could bring him down were a few old vets—warrant officers and non-coms all—while he was one of the movers and shakers in Washington."

"Yeah, well, my money would always be on the grunts," Jack Davis said. "There was no glory for those who survived our war. No accolades. No yellow ribbons. We just came home and went about living the rest of our lives as well as we could. Most of us tried to forget the things we'd seen. I'm glad Vince Morelli had the courage to stand up and say that some of them needed to be remembered."

Like his recitation of the incident in his office that day, Davis's words made enough of an impact on his audience to hold them silent for a few seconds. It was Cara who broke the stillness.

"Get well soon," she said, stepping forward to hold out her hand to the pilot. "And thank you for telling me something about my father. Now that he's gone, every bit of information I learn about him seems more precious."

She bent and put her lips against his forehead. When she stepped back, there was a flush of color along the top of the older man's cheeks.

"Thanks for what you said about my dad," Nick said. "And for helping me understand the demons that drove him."

He would always regret that he hadn't known before his death what had happened to his father. His emotions were now tinged more with sadness than with anger over their relationship. Maybe now he could finally come to terms with the distance his dad had maintained between them. At the least he could now understand it more.

"He was a good man when it mattered," Davis said. "Whatever else you remember about him, you remember that."

Nick nodded, fighting an unexpected sting behind his eyes.

"I suspect the staff is ready to throw all of us out. We did promise we wouldn't tire you. It was an honor to meet you, Mr. Davis," Griff said, moving toward the bed to shake hands.

He turned and started toward the door, holding it open for Ainsworth. Nick and Cara followed the executive assistant director out into the corridor.

"Ms. Simonson," Griff said, taking her hand. "If you ever decide that technology is boring, we can always use another quality operative at the Phoenix," he said with a smile.

"If I learned anything during the last few days, it's that I'm not cut out for the kind of work you and Nick do. I prefer my challenges to be the intellectual kind— and less dangerous."

Griff laughed, releasing her hand before he turned to Nick. "Take some time to unwind. There's nothing going on at the agency right now that we can't handle."

"I don't know if I can ever tell you how much I appreciate everything that the Phoenix—"

"Then don't try. Nobody there is looking for gratitude. You would have—and have—done the same for anyone there. We know that, and so do you. As I said, take a few days."

He smiled at Cara again before he turned and walked down the hospital corridor to where Ainsworth was waiting. Heads together, the two of them stood before the bank of elevators, obviously still talking about the implications of the events of the last few days.

"Are you going to take him up on his offer?" Cara asked.

Nick pulled his gaze from the two men to look down into her eyes. They reflected the same emotional exhaustion he felt.

"Probably not. I've left the agency shorthanded long enough. What about you? Are you going back to Orvid?"

"I don't know. I feel as if…" She closed her mouth, her eyes searching his face.

"As if what?"

"As if I haven't had time enough to grieve. Or to remember the good things. As silly as it sounds, what Jack said about my father looking as if he were going to be sick as soon as they took off… I don't know. I guess I always thought of him as being old. And he wasn't. At one time he was that green kid riding in Jack's chopper."

And at one time Nick's father had been a sergeant who witnessed a wartime atrocity and had never forgotten it. He wasn't sure that was a memory he wanted to savor.

"Take some more time," he said. "Your boss will understand."

"Like yours?"

Her eyes said far more, but he knew she wouldn't put it into words. She had too much pride for that.

Whatever happened between them, he would have to be the one who initiated it. That was okay with him. He liked being in control. Except this time…

"Griff reminded me of something I'd forgotten."

"What's that?" she asked, the hope he'd seen in her eyes changing to puzzlement.

"There's a beach house we sometimes use. It's pretty far off the beaten track. Isolated on top of this hill that looks down on the ocean. There are windows across the back so that no matter where you are inside, you can see the beach."

There was a small flare of the same emotion he'd seen before, but it was a long heartbeat before she responded to his description. "It sounds lovely."

"I don't think anyone is using it right now."

Another beat of silence, and then she shook her head. "I'm not sure… I told you I'm not good at intelligence work. If there's something here I'm supposed to be figuring out…"

"I thought we might take advantage of his offer."

"Griff's offer of the house?" she clarified carefully.

"Unless you really *do* want to go back to work tomorrow."

Still holding his eyes, she shook her head again. "No. Not necessarily. They've managed without me this long…"

"Obviously they're better men than I am."

"I don't…" Her lips closed again, stopping the question, but her eyes clung to his.

"Because I'm not sure I can do that anymore."

This time the silence stretched through several seconds.

"Manage…without me?"

"It might be something we need to talk about."

"At this...beach house."

"That's what I had in mind. What do you think?"

"I'll need to call my mother."

There was something about the idea of her calling Miriam to tell her about his proposition that struck Nick as funny. He laughed. "Just as long as you don't invite her to join us."

She smiled, sharing his amusement. "She was coming to stay with me. I just need to ask her to postpone her visit."

"You have your phone?"

"You should do that more often," she said as she looked down to pull it from of the outside pocket of her purse.

"Do what? Invite you to come away with me?"

"Laugh. I've never heard you laugh before."

"Call your mother. Tell her you aren't going to be home for a few days, and we'll see what we can do about that."

"About...laughing?"

"Maybe it's time we tried it for a change of pace. What do you think?"

"I think that if I did ask my mom for permission to go away with you, she'd probably be overjoyed. But just in case..." She smiled at him before she began punching in her aunt's number.

A safe house somewhere in Virginia

Nick awoke to find the place beside him empty. For one heart-stopping moment the nightmares he had spent the last week trying to erase were back in his head.

Then he remembered that it was over. Whatever the reason Cara had for leaving their bed, it had nothing to do with the people who had hunted them as they had hunted their fathers' murderer.

He threw the sheet off his lower body and sat up, his eyes scanning the upstairs bedroom. The door to the hall was open, and despite the predawn darkness, it was clear there was no one else in the room.

A quick survey of the other rooms on the second level found them empty, as well. In the days they'd spent here, they had gone for a couple of late night swims. He began to worry that Cara might have ventured out onto the beach alone.

As isolated as the house was, there was no need to worry about someone else being out there. It was simply that, after all that had happened, he wasn't comfortable with the idea of her being there alone.

Or anywhere else, he acknowledged.

His bare feet made no sound as he hurried down the stairs and across the worn wooden floors of the lower level. The rooms he looked into on his way to the back of the house were deserted in the waning moonlight.

He had almost passed the entrance to the kitchen, when out of the corner of his eye he noticed a shape, little more than a silhouette, against that room's wide wall of glass. Cara was standing perfectly still in front of the darkened windows, looking out on the ocean below.

Although he had thrown on the shorts he'd worn today before he'd left the bedroom, she was still nude. Her body as beautifully elemental as when he'd made love to her before they had drifted off to sleep locked in one another's arms.

"Cara?"

She turned to smile at him over her shoulder. Welcoming him to join her in whatever she was doing.

"What's wrong?" he asked as he walked across the expanse of tile that separated them.

"This is my favorite time of day here," she said, looking out again at the panorama of monochromatic sky and sea. "These last few minutes before dawn. I didn't want to miss them."

They had acknowledged yesterday that however much they desired it, neither of them could stretch this idyllic interlude to another day. They would pack up the few things they'd brought with them this morning and return to Washington.

Neither of them had said much after the decision had been reached. Nick had been unable to tell her how he felt about the days they'd spent together as he'd made love to her tonight.

He couldn't afford to think about this being over. About not waking up next to her and having her turn into his arms, putting her face against his shoulder. Holding her while she slept. Eating breakfast at the small table set in front of the windows where she was now standing. Watching her as she ran joyfully to meet him on the stretch of sand below. Laughing together at the antics of the gulls they had fed at sunset.

Laughter. That was something else she had given him. Along with honesty and the gift of her intellect. All the qualities he had come to value in the two short weeks he'd known her.

"We'll come back," he said, putting his hands around her upper arms.

"It won't be the same."

"Why not?" He bent to touch his lips to the softness beneath her jawline.

She leaned her head against the side of his, a strand of silken hair catching in the roughness of his whiskers.

"I don't know. I'm being stupid. Being a woman," she said with a laugh.

She turned into his embrace, her breasts pressing against his bare chest. It was a sensation that, despite the number of times they'd made love, had an instant and dramatic effect. She leaned back to look up into his face.

"But I'm going to miss *this,*" she said, her lips tilting upward.

"The house?" he teased.

"That, too."

She put the side of her face against his chest, her hands resting on the tops of his shoulders. He slipped his arms around her waist, drawing her nearer.

"I can't do anything about the house," he said. At the enormity of what he was about to do, his heart had begun to beat so heavily he knew she must feel it. There was a knot of anxiety in his stomach, but he forced himself to go on. "But there's no reason that the rest should end."

She was so still that he wondered if she'd heard him. Of course, the only other sound in the kitchen was the muted crash of the waves against the shore below. Finally she lifted her head, looking up into his face. She was no longer smiling.

"*If* you don't want it to," he added, simply because he didn't know how to answer what was in her eyes.

"What do *you* want?"

You. Every night. In my arms. And every day...

He had never allowed himself to think that far. Not until now.

"I don't want this to end, either," he managed.

He had expected her to make it easy, once he confessed that much, but still she said nothing, looking up into his eyes.

"*I* have a house," he said to break her waiting silence. "It isn't as scenic as this one. Actually it isn't even mine. I just live there."

She knew all that. He was making a fool of himself. All he needed to say...

"It's empty. It's always so damned empty." *Like my life, except for the Phoenix. And one day...* "I don't want to end up bitter and alone. I don't want to end up like my father."

As he watched, her eyes glazed with moisture. She controlled the tears, smiling at him as she put her hand along the side of his face.

"No," she whispered. "No."

He couldn't tell if the word was meant as comfort or sympathy or refusal, but now that he'd begun, he knew that he had to finish this. If he didn't, no matter the outcome, he knew he would regret it for the rest of his life.

"My mother left him when I was eight. She couldn't live with it anymore. I never blamed her for that, but…I guess I'm saying…I don't know much about how this is supposed to work."

She shook her head, a crease forming between her brows. "How what's supposed to work, Nick?"

Again his heart rate accelerated, as if he were about to embark on some dangerous mission. Like all the ones he'd been involved in since he was eighteen.

Except this time, he had no training. No idea what to expect.

"Marriage," he said, almost dreading what he would see in her face in response.

Her lips closed, and the soft gleam of tears was back in her eyes. "Are you asking me to marry you?"

"I know I'm a very bad risk…." he began and then ground to a stop.

"And I've never been a risk taker…"

The too-rapid beat of his heart faltered as his words had.

"But…if I've learned anything from all this," she went on, "it's that courage is doing what you know is right, even if you're afraid."

He let the words echo in his head, trying to make sure they meant what he'd thought they did. "Is that a yes?"

"Absolutely, Nick Morelli," she said, smiling up at him before she put her arms around his neck and pulled his head down so that her mouth could reach his.

"Absolutely," she whispered again, just before his lips closed over hers.

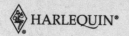
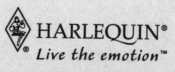

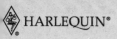
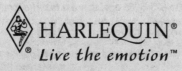

HARLEQUIN *Super*ROMANCE®

Seattle after Midnight
by C.J. Carmichael
(Superromance #1240)
On sale November 2004

"Hello, Seattle. Welcome to 'Georgia after Midnight,' the show for lonely hearts and lovers…."

P.I. Pierce Harding can't resist listening to Georgia Lamont's late-night radio show. Something about her sultry voice calls to him. But Georgia has also attracted an unwanted listener, one who crosses the line between fan and fanatic. When the danger escalates, Pierce knows that he will do anything to keep Georgia safe. Even risk his heart…

Available wherever Harlequin books are sold

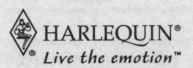

HARLEQUIN®
Live the emotion™

www.eHarlequin.com